D0921145

PORTABLE BLACK MAGIC

OC 22 '19

This book is a work of fiction. The names, characters, places and incidents are products of the author's imagination or have been used fictitiously and are not to be construed as real. Any resemblance to persons, living or dead, actual events, locales or organizations is entirely coincidental.

"Where Would We Be If We Couldn't Tweet Our Thoughts?" was originally published as "Instagram Baby" by *Ariel Chart* (2018), "Talons" was originally published by both *Poppy Road Review* and *X-R-A-Y Literary Magazine* (2018), and "The Salvatore Grant" was originally published by *Literally Stories* (2018).

© 2019 Randolph Walker, Jr.
Image by Jonny Lindner (Creative Commons)

All rights are reserved. No part of this book may be used or reproduced in any manner whatsoever without written permission from the author. The author may be reached via his website, www.ranwalker.com.

10 9 8 7 6 5 4 3 2 1

ISBN 9781020001000

First Edition Paperback

Library of Congress Control Number: 2019910748

45 Alternate Press, LLC
Hampton, Virginia

PORTABLE BLACK MAGIC

Tales of the Afro Strange

RAN WALKER

CONTENTS

In memory of my dear friend and mentor,
Dr. Lloren A. Foster

SECRET ROOMS IN THE MANSIONS OF MY MIND

"Every portrait that is painted with feeling is a portrait of the artist, not of the sitter."
~ *Oscar Wilde*

A pollo awakened to the sobriety of reality dawning over him. The dreams were *hyperrealistic*, yet surrealistic in the way dreams often are, but one thing was always the same: *she* was in them. No name. Just a vision of explicit pulchritude that seemed to explode into his periphery from every direction. Sometimes she would hold his face gently in her hands and press her lips to his. Other times she would pull him into her, the warmth of her legs wrapped around his waist, her body enveloping him like some plush glove molded perfectly to fit his 6'3" frame. Regardless of how she came to him, he would awaken at first ecstatic, before the dull ache of reality settled over him and he realized she was only a figment of his imagination, a perfection that only existed somewhere deep within his subconscious.

Apollo sat on the edge of his bed and stretched his arms

wildly in different directions. He was alone, which was perfectly
fine by him, though there were days when Anita would stay the
night and ease some of the monotony that accompanied his
living in a loft in the Bearden District of The City. Their arrangement was simple and convenient: they would sleep with each
other on occasion and hang out, a casual "Netflix and chill"
scenario, with the understanding that should either of them find
something outside of their arrangement that was more promising,
they would move on. So far their arrangement had lasted a year,
which suited Apollo fine, but he sensed that Anita was tiring of
the situation. She'd even been privy to some of his more amorous
dreams of the woman who had come to undermine his conscious
dalliances.

His cell phone rang, and he reached for it, not surprised to
see Anita's name on the ID.

"Hello?"

"Hey, Apollo. We need to talk. Are you gonna be around this
morning?"

"Yeah," he responded, confused. "You sure you don't want to
talk right now?"

He didn't know what was on her mind, but the words "we
need to talk" had never yielded anything positive to anyone, as
far as he knew.

"I'd rather us talk face-to-face. Can I come over?"

"Sure."

"See you in a bit."

"Okay."

As Apollo tossed the phone back on his bed, he took a deep
breath to quell the hammering of his heartbeat. *Could she be pregnant?* he wondered, an overwhelming sense of dread forming in
his stomach.

He walked across the cool floor, feeling the imperfections of
paint splatters across the wood against the balls of his feet. The

bathroom sat off to the side, small but suitable for someone like himself, someone who found beauty in the miniaturization of things. He started the hot water in the walk-in shower and quickly disrobed. There was no point in drawing it out in hopes that Anita would join him. He suspected whatever she had to share with him would have diminished his morning libido anyway.

As the water splashed across his face, he reminded himself to breathe. There was nothing to worry about until there was something to worry about. At this point everything was beyond his control, so patience would have to be his best friend.

Once he finished drying off, he tossed on a white t-shirt that, while it was clean, still bore paint flecks, as did the jeans he put on. His artwork leaned against various points along the wall, two easels of different sizes spaced out just off the main walking path of the loft. Only one of the easels had a canvas resting upon it, and that canvas was bare, the exact condition it had been when he purchased it from the art supply store. It had been that way for two weeks now while he worked out several sketches in his notebook, and he was slowly starting to wonder if he was delaying the beginning of this new piece because of some unconscious fear. He just hoped Anita was not about to deliver that fear to his doorstep.

She lived across town, far enough away that they had to make a concerted effort to see each other. They didn't shop at the same grocery stores or corner bodegas. He had only met her because he accidentally spilled a drink on her at one of The Internet's concerts and had offered to buy her drinks for the rest of the night. After alcohol and conversations about alternative soul music and the state of Black cinema, they found themselves drenched in sweat, their nude bodies sliding back and forth like a record on Grandmaster Flash's turntable.

In the following weeks, both now completely sober, their

worlds continued to unfold in a comfortable rhythm. The fact that what they shared never went beyond hanging out and having sex didn't bother Apollo, and he figured it didn't bother Anita either, as she never brought it up. In fact, the only conversation they'd ever had about committed relationships was when she proposed they just give a heads-up to the other should something more serious jump off elsewhere. He'd nodded his agreement.

He enjoyed his solitude and space. He viewed his art as an insatiable mistress and felt that it would be unfair to place a woman in a position to have to contend with that.

Now Anita wanted to have a talk about something that was apparently important enough that she would catch an Uber across town on her one day off from the theater. She was in her third month of a new show, with Monday as the designated black day. Apollo smiled for a moment when he remembered that Garfield, the cartoon character created by Jim Davis, hated Mondays, too. The brief moment of levity dissipated almost as quickly as it started when he heard the firm raps against the other side of his front door.

๑๛๛

ANITA WALKED in and quickly made her way to the bed at the edge of the room, taking a seat near the foot.

"You all right?" he asked, walking over and standing directly in front of her, his legs feeling as though they were encased in huge blocks of concrete.

"I just wanted to tell you this face-to-face."

He took a deep breath and waited.

"We have to end this," she said.

He listened silently, waiting for her to tell him about the child she was carrying, *his child*, but she didn't add anything additional to her declaration. Surely this wasn't it, he thought. She could have told him that much over the phone.

To help push her along, he asked, "What's wrong?"

"I met someone."

Again, he sighed, this time out of relief. So he wouldn't be a father after all. He felt almost devious in his thoughts, but he wanted to at least be attentive to Anita's needs, especially since it weighed heavily enough on her thoughts for her to make the trip across town to tell him this.

"Tell me what happened."

This time Anita took a deep breath. It was clear she felt she might be hurting his feelings, and that notion warmed his heart. She wanted him to mourn what they had had. He owed her that much, he figured.

"He's a film producer from Los Angeles. I'll be moving out there in a few days."

The part of him that viewed her as his "homey/lover/friend" wanted to tell her how cliché all of that sounded, and that any description of a significant other that started with a description of what he did for a living was surely destined to fail in time—but what was the point? He had learned from his father once upon a time that it was not fair to strip a woman of her beliefs if he had nothing to offer in replacement. As much as he would miss having her around from time to time, he was not prepared to offer more of himself than he already had.

"Do you have anything to say?" she asked him, her voice begin to rise in its incredulity. "You're going to let me walk away?"

"I'm confused," he admitted. "I thought you were telling that me you had already decided to leave me to be with this other dude."

"You know what? You're right. I just wanted to at least tell you to your face, and I've done just that." She rose from the bed and began to walk toward the door.

"Hold up," he said, still trying to figure out what had caused the temperature in the room to shift. "Give me a second. I'm still processing things."

She stopped, standing still by the door. This was her way of yielding to what would amount to a romantic counter-offer, but Apollo, still searching himself, could find no reason to stand in her way.

"I thought what we had was good," he finally said.

"Yeah. But you don't really want to be with me *seriously*," she said. "If you even showed any genuine interest in me, I wouldn't have even been able to get close to anyone else."

"But you told me that you wanted to be casual, that *this* was supposed to be us just having fun," he responded.

"I just said that so you wouldn't feel pressure to be in a relationship with me. I thought you knew that, but I guess I wasn't clear enough."

Apollo lowered his head, considering her words for the first time. "I didn't know."

"You didn't want to know," she responded. "I can't fall in love with you knowing you'll never love me back. I'm just not built that way." Placing her hand against his chest, she continued. "I don't know where this relationship in Cali will lead, but I'm not getting any younger. I can't just stand still with you when I can be moving forward."

He didn't know what to say, so he said nothing.

"Well, it's been real," Anita said. "Have a good life."

Although her words were likely intended to be abrasive, Apollo offered her well wishes and was surprised when she accepted his embrace.

They stood by the door holding each other, and Apollo,

wondering if there was still any magic left between them, leaned down to kiss her neck.

"See. You only want me like *this*. You don't really care about me."

"How can you say that? We were so cool with each other."

She looked at him quizzically. "I'm too old to be *cool* with someone. And, Apollo, so are you."

Even in the half hour after she left, he found himself still standing by the door, confused and a bit hurt—and if he allowed himself to completely steel his mind and relinquish his phantom shame, he felt a deep and resonant relief.

☙❧

THERE WERE TIMES WHEN, as an artist, Apollo allowed his attention to become focused on a particular color. Before he met Anita, he found himself insatiable when it came to the color blue. For months he obsessed over cerulean and then Prussian blue. Then there was the week he painted nearly nonstop, convinced the answer to life came from Yves Klein and that it was Apollo's responsibility to share with the world the importance of blue. The speakers in his loft were bathed in Miles Davis's *Kind of Blue*, particularly the song "All Blues." To have called this moment in time Apollo's "Blue Period," would have been an understatement, as he had strongly considered never using another color again.

Then one day he woke up and blue no longer held the same appeal for him. It was like that moment in *The Wiz* where the wizard all of a sudden changed the color the dancers had been celebrating. It was then that he stared at his blank canvas (as he did now) and wondered what would happen next.

His teaching job at the local design college financed the loft, but he was working feverishly now that the summer break had arrived, eager to complete art for the exhibition he had scheduled in late July. This was his first major show, the result of years of cultivating a relationship with the Northmore Gallery downtown. It would be a one-man show over the course of one week. He had thrown everything he had at this show, but lately he had become underwhelmed with the pieces he had selected, the same pieces that had originally helped score him the show. He was determined to create new pieces that at least reflected his current state of mind, but he had come to find over the past two weeks that his mind was as blank as the canvas before him.

If the show was successful, he could hopefully sign with an artist agent who would then open more doors for him. Apollo didn't mind teaching, but he knew that if he could make a living creating art, that would be preferable to helping young students who likely stumbled into his class as an elective for a different major. Sometimes he thought about his vocation in the way that a racecar driver might think of having to drive a school bus. He was meant to create, to explore his craft at high speeds, at tremendous depths, and teaching students didn't allow him the opportunity to release the throttle and really let loose. Still it was a paycheck with benefits, so until he could make a name for himself as an artist, he would do what he had to do.

He stared at the blank canvas for another hour before deciding to return to sleep. Remnants of Anita's departure still played in the back of his mind and for some reason manifested themselves as a painful pulsing just behind his eyelids. A nap might cure that, he thought, lying down on his bed and sinking his head into the pillow. And if he were lucky—really lucky—maybe the woman in his dreams would return to him, offering him the kind of solace only she could offer.

THIS DREAM BEGAN the way his dreams often began: he was

standing in the lobby of a massive hotel that seemed to meander in every direction. The people scattered across the lobby were dressed formally, but he stood there in a t-shirt and jeans, his sneakers accented with dried flecks of paint. For some reason he knew he had to get to the eleventh floor, maybe because he had once lived on the eleventh floor of a building shortly after he finished college. He rushed to find the closest elevator and once he boarded it, he searched among the many buttons for the one labeled "11."

A few other people boarded the elevator poking buttons for various floors. While Apollo waited for the elevator door to close, he glanced at the back of the elevator, which was a clear glass that allowed him to see the city beyond the hotel. Then the elevator began to rise, a bit too quickly for his comfort. Suddenly the box began to tilt, causing everyone in the elevator to cling to the sides of the box to avoid falling down. The elevator made a sharp stop before zooming sideways at a speed far faster than the speed of its ascent.

Apollo felt his legs weaken, as he began praying the elevator would not drop. Not able to stand the idea of the elevator violently dropping from a height that already made him uncomfortable, a height that was surely above the eleventh floor, he exited the elevator as soon as the doors opened. Even in his dreams, he was not cut out for this kind of Wonka Great Glass Elevator scenario. The floor number read 14B, and after walking a few feet it became clear why there was a "B" designation. Almost as if dropped at a slightly different and seemingly disconnected level lay 14A. He had no clue how to navigate 14B or 14A, let alone how to get to the eleventh floor.

When he managed to find the exit door leading to the stairwell, his confusion continued unabated. The stairs not only went up and down, but they went up and down at angles that totally confused his ability to tell exactly where he was. The stairwell reminded him of the stairwell from his middle school—except on steroids—as if he had entered an entirely different hotel altogether.

He stood still, not knowing exactly where to go. He picked the stairwell going downward and to the right and began trying to count the floors. There would be no thirteenth floor, so the next floor down would be twelve and the one after that eleven. He opened the door and found himself back in the hotel, the halls seeming to stretch on forever.

What room was he looking for?

1105. It was the number that appeared in his head, so he went with it.

He ran down the hall towards 1105, and once he reached it, he reached for his key card in his pocket, only to find out that it was not there. He knocked. Why? He didn't know. It just seemed like the right thing to do.

The door opened and there was a guy standing there.

"Apollo," the guy said, standing in the doorway in a pair of boxers and a t-shirt, "she moved your stuff down to 403."

"Who moved my things?" he responded.

"Some girl." The guy, edging the door closed, glanced back. "Hey, dude, I have to get back to something, if you catch my drift."

"Yeah. No problem," Apollo said, stepping back.

403. He would have to head down to 403.

Not trusting the elevators, he searched again for a stairwell and began the process of running down the stairs, all with the hope that he hadn't somehow wound up in another building entirely.

When he emerged from the stairwell, he was on the fourth floor right next to 403. He quickly knocked on the door.

"Coming," a soft voice on the other side of the door said.

The door opened slowly, and standing there in a sheer

negligee, her curly afro framing her face like rays around the sun, was Apollo's dream woman, her face clearer than anything he had ever laid eyes on in a conscious state.

"It's you," he said, breathlessly.

"Yes. I've been waiting for you."

He stepped closer to her, and she met him, pressing herself against him. He could feel the warmth and softness of her breasts through the negligee.

"Why can't you be real?" he said, leaning in to kiss her waiting lips.

She placed a tender hand against his chest, not to stop him, but to encourage him. "Who says that I'm not?"

Her kiss pulled him into a deep cobalt space, and as his body yielded to her, colored petals of salmon pink, blood orange, and gold burst against the background framing them into an eroticized version of a Kehinde Wiley painting.

She was perfect, he knew, and as he fought the urge to open his eyes from this dream, he knew he could never be happy with any woman knowing that she awaited him in his dreams.

But as he was unable to fight his growing consciousness and realization that he was no longer asleep, he regretfully rose from his bed. This was the second time that day that he felt a pang of loss.

He looked around his loft, and the loneliness that had not been there before, mainly because he knew that Anita was there if he needed her, had somehow encroached upon his peace of mind, and he was left only with the desire to cure that loneliness.

He stared at his phone, debating with himself if he should apologize to Anita and have her come back. He knew what she wanted to hear. He could tell her those things, offer her those reassurances to fight the emptiness he was feeling, but he knew he wouldn't do that. Not because there wasn't a part of him that wanted to do just that; he just knew that Anita deserved far more than he could offer. He couldn't deprive her of having a chance at happiness by keeping her hostage with his on indecision. Instead, he stared at the blank canvas that, at this point, seemed to have become one with the easel, as if it would never be anything he could rest against the wall like his other pieces.

He sat in the chair before the easel and closed his eyes. He could still see the face of the woman from his dreams. When he opened his eyes, he reached for one of his *F* pencils and leaned forward. He would capture her face as best he could.

If he did a good job, at least he could look at her face and never feel the loneliness that had recently come to set up home in his loft.

ONCE HE HAD COMPLETED the painting, he stared at it, unable to believe she now existed in his conscious space. She was breathtakingly beautiful, and her eyes seemed to call to him like they had many times before in his dreams. He had painted her in the window of a tall hotel, the only visible face, yet she was there, in all her splendor. When he looked at that painting against the backdrop of his other pieces, he could see an incredible contrast. It wasn't just that it was *her*; the painting was actually *better* than the others.

Inspired, Apollo went out and bought several more canvases of varying sizes and brought them home. As he stared at the white of each canvas, his mind began to swim with images of his new muse. Turning on Coltrane's *A Love Supreme* in his studio speakers, he picked up the first canvas and began to sketch. This time he drew a more focused picture of her, as if she had been in his loft sitting for a portrait. Strictly from the memories of his dreams, he recreated her portrait and began to slowly add in the acrylic colors. Her likeness was so life-like that he sat staring at her for what felt like hours. He had rendered her so realistically and three dimensionally that he felt as though he might be able to reach into the painting and hold her in his arms.

Once he finished that painting, he placed it against the wall to dry alongside the others. He reached for another canvas, and, within minutes, he had begun to sketch her in another position. For the next five days, Apollo did nothing but eat, sleep, and paint his muse. When he was not dreaming of her, he was painting her. Never had he been so inspired or feverishly obsessed with his work. This would surely be the work he would use for his show. He had never painted anything as well as he had his muse, and the idea of sharing his artwork with the world pleased him immensely.

In the midst of his painting, he forced himself to take a moment to call Cesar Neddleton, the gallery owner, to share the latest updates on his exhibition.

"Cesar, you have to see them," he said, breathlessly.

"I'm pretty busy until three this afternoon. I can swing by for a few minutes and see what you've got."

"Thanks."

When he hung up the phone, Apollo took some of the older paintings he had originally planned to use for his show and placed them against the wall at the far end of the room. The various portraits of his muse now exclusively occupied the dominant space of his work area. They were lined up sequentially in the order in which they were painted, starting with the hotel. He stood back, admiring them. They didn't just satisfy his artistic judgment; they made him happy. He had taken someone who meant so much to him in one dimension of his mind and had brought her into the space in which he lived and did his art. It wasn't the easiest thing he had done, but it was by far the most rewarding. As he took in the twelve pieces he had painted, he once again felt a glow of relief settle over him, as he knew, even with the open relationship he had had with Anita, she would not have gone for seeing how this other woman had taken over his studio. She had wanted more from him, and the problem was that Apollo found the woman in his dreams for more alluring than Anita. It was not fair to her that his imagination should limit their involvement. It made little sense to him, and he doubted it would have made *any* sense to anyone else.

Yet, there he stood in his loft, a smile stretched across his face so wide that he could simply lean forward and fall into his own happiness.

He quickly showered and tossed on a t-shirt and jeans. He was still spitting toothpaste from his mouth when the buzzer from downstairs signaled Cesar's arrival. He rinsed out his mouth and gargled after clicking the buzzer letting him in.

By the time Cesar knocked on the door of the actual loft, Apollo was clean and fresh-faced, his breath still minty. He was in a good mood, eager to show off his new pieces to the one person who could help jumpstart the kind of career he hoped to have.

He opened the door, and Cesar stepped into the room in the smooth way of a person used to viewing beautiful things. Cesar was dressed in a seersucker suit with a bowtie. His frohawk, which had been dyed almost the same color as his golden skin complexion, made him look like at least a million and a half dollars. But Apollo knew the game; they were all strivers, and he knew that Cesar's gallery relied on painters like him to appeal to a certain segment of the upwardly mobile African-American art collecting population. There were many levels of art business above where Cesar stood, but one wouldn't know it by simply looking at him.

"Glad you could stop by," Apollo said, shaking Cesar's hand and ending it with a dap. Yes, they were in the business of art, but they were still Black men who were heavily tied to their culture and had no intention of changing that aspect of who they were.

"No problem. Jackson Parks is down in the gallery right now setting up his exhibition for this coming week. You should go down and check it out when you get a minute. He's got some really provocative stuff going on."

"Sure thing. But first I wanted to update you one what I've been working on."

As they moved across the room, Apollo began by telling him the story of how he had lost his mojo for a while, as he tried to assemble pieces for his own exhibition, but then he started to paint the woman from his dreams.

He was still in the middle of his story when they reached the paintings lining the wall and Cesar interrupted him. "This is a joke right?"

"What do you mean?" Apollo responded, unable to conceal his hurt.

"You and Jackson are doing some millennial take on Fanny Eaton, right?"

"Who is Fanny Eaton?"

"The Black woman the Pre-Raphaelites were painting."

Apollo had never heard of Fanny Eaton and knew next to nothing about the Pre-Raphaelites. Art history was such an enormous thing, and one only knew about that from which his or her greatest inspirations had come.

Apollo stared at his paintings. They were perfect. He had no idea what the hell Cesar was talking about and told him as much.

"I feel like I'm seeing this woman everywhere. You've definitely got to come down to the gallery and see what Jackson's been doing."

"You mean he painted the same woman?"

"I'm pretty sure it's the same woman. Beautiful Afro goddess.

Exact same nose and lips. Eyes are identical. Yep. He's painted her."

"So she's real?" Apollo asked, his heartbeat racing.

"I would imagine so. And if you dreamed her, it was probably because you saw her somewhere."

It was all too much for Apollo to take in, so he sat down on the stool near his empty easel. He didn't know what to say. He was completely dumbfounded. When he was finally able to find his voice, he said, "So Jackson is down at the gallery right now?"

"Yep. I just left him."

"Can I go back with you to meet him and see his work?"

"Sure. From what I'm seeing here, you guys have a lot in common."

Apollo tossed on a pair of black leather loafers to go over his bare feet and a thin black cotton blazer. He reached for his bowler hat as the two men left the loft and headed down the elevator and out of the building.

❧

THE GALLERY WAS ROUGHLY four blocks away, on the outer edge of the Bearden Art District, so the walk only took minutes. Apollo was eager to arrive, but he didn't want to outpace Cesar, whose leisurely strides seemed aimed at a kind of ease and nonchalance.

When they arrived and stepped through the door, there was a slight partition designed to create an air of mystery for what lay behind it. This was where people would be admitted, but just beyond the partition was a wide-open space, and when Apollo and Cesar walked into that open space, Apollo nearly fell to his knees as he took in the paintings of his muse scattered around the room. A guy with brilliant orange dreadlocks, the color of an autumn that had not yet arrived, sat on a small blanket in the middle of the room, eating a homemade turkey and cheese sandwich. He immediately perked up and waved at Cesar, slowly rising to his feet.

Placing the remains of his sandwich back into a paper bag that rested on the blanket and wiping his hands against the sides of his dungarees, he waved again.

"Jack, it's looking good in here," Cesar said, gesturing around the space. "There's someone I want you to meet," he added. "This is Apollo. He's got an exhibition here in a few weeks."

Apollo stepped forward to shake Jackson's hand, but Jackson offered him a pound instead.

"Just finished eating lunch," Jackson added, once again wiping his hands on his pants.

"Hey. No problem," Apollo responded.

Now he openly looked around the space, taking the totality of it all in. "Wow. This is pretty impressive."

"Jack," Cesar said, tracing his fingertips along the lapels of his coat, "I was telling Apollo that he had to meet you because the two of you have a lot in common."

"Really?" Jackson said. "What are you working on?" he said to Apollo.

Apollo took a deep breath before he answered. "I've been painting this woman I've been dreaming about. Honestly, she's kind of taken over my work."

"Hey, I totally understand that. We're artists, and artists can't deny the muse."

In that single moment, Apollo bristled slightly, almost imperceptibly, but it was there for anyone used to analyzing the subtlest nuances of human gestures. It was the word "muse" that shook him. He felt as if the woman painted on the canvases around the gallery was *his* muse, and he was not willing to share her with anyone else, no matter how ridiculous such a concept was.

"The woman in your paintings," Apollo started, pacing

himself as to not come across as abrasive, "is the woman I have been dreaming about."

"Really?" Jackson said. It seemed to be a word that he enjoyed using. "That's Akira."

"You mean she's a real person."

"Oh definitely."

"And you know her?"

"Yep. She posed for this art class I took in Atlanta a few years ago. She had that *look*, you know, that *je ne sais quoi*."

Apollo could feel his heart racing, but he kept his voice steady. "So she's a model."

"She was, the last time I saw her." Jackson looked around at his artwork. "And you've never seen her in person?"

"No. Only in my dreams. And, here's the kicker: my entire exhibit is centered around her—well, it was until I saw your work."

"Come on, man. Don't do that," Jackson said. "We're artists. You have to showcase the stuff that moves your soul. It doesn't matter if we've painted the same woman."

Apollo nodded slowly, still taking it all in.

"Hey," Jackson said empathetically, "if it's okay with you, can I see your pieces?"

Apollo tried to shake the haze clouding his head. *Akira.* The name flowed through his mind like honey drizzling down a model on the cover of an Ohio Players' album cover.

"Sure," he finally said.

Now that he knew Akira was real, he felt a slow pang beginning to build inside of him. It was a desire that had not existed until that moment: he wanted to meet her.

JACKSON STARED at the paintings along the wall of Apollo's loft, his head tilting from left to right.

"I don't know," he said, "but I kind of thought maybe there would be some similarities, not something this spot-on. This is *definitely* Akira. And you've never seen her before?"

Apollo shook his head. "Only in my dreams."

Jackson shivered slightly, as if being chilled by a breeze. "That's some freaky shit! You got me weirded out, man."

"How do you think *I* felt when I saw *your* exhibit?" Apollo said, chuckling uneasily.

Jackson leaned in closer to the paintings, examining them from different angles. "You're pretty talented, man. I don't normally gas up other artists, but you've got some skills."

"Thanks," Apollo responded. "Your work is pretty dope, too."

"It's a'ight," Jackson said playfully.

Apollo stared at the images before them. "Can you tell me more about her?" It was the most controlled way he could think to broach the subject directly.

Jackson's eyes moved from canvas to canvas, eventually reaching the first painting of Akira in the hotel. "Wow! This one is really something," he said, pointing. Then, as if remembering the question, he said, "Man, I was studying at the Southwest Atlanta Institute of the Arts, and this girl just came in one day. She was the first sista to model for the group. I remember thinking, I'm gonna paint the shit out of this girl."

"So it was a Life Art class?" Apollo asked, trying to suppress the jealousy he felt from Jackson having possibly seen Akira nude.

"Yeah," Jackson responded. Then, sensing Apollo's discomfort, he added, "Hey, it was just art."

Apollo smiled, a bit too uneasily. "Yeah. I know. Just wrapping my mind around the fact that she's a real person, I guess."

"True dat. And she's still out there, somewhere in the world."

"Do you remember her last name?"

Jackson twisted one of his orange dreadlocks in his fingers, as he considered this. "Nah. Actually, I'm not sure she ever referred to herself as anything other than Akira. Maybe you could google her first name and 'life art model' to see what comes up."

It was as if a light bulb had gone off in Apollo's head. Why hadn't he considered that? "Jack, you're a genius!"

"Ah, man, it's nothing if not true," he said, laughing at his own joke.

Apollo walked across the room to his desk, and Jackson followed. The two of them hovered over his open MacBook awaiting the results of the search. Nothing useful came up, only images of the manga character of the same name and the occasional pencil sketch. There was no image that remotely resembled the Akira who had so totally taken over Apollo's creativity.

"I don't know what to say," Jackson said, shrugging. "But I know she's out there somewhere."

"Yeah."

"Hey, Apollo, I've got to get back to the gallery. Thanks for letting me check out your work."

"No problem," he responded. "I appreciate you hearing me out. I'm still trying to make sense of all of this."

"I get it, man. Believe me. I do."

"So when is your show?" Apollo asked.

"It starts next week. You should come through."

Apollo nodded. "Don't worry. I'll be there."

The two artists dapped each other, and Apollo showed Jackson out.

When he returned to his loft, Apollo stared at the images of Akira before him. He then returned to his computer and began doing every variation of search he could for that name until he grew tired and fell into a deep slumber.

⚜

THE GENTLE BREEZE of an April night danced across Apollo's face as he stood in some large nature park, only the moonlight above him providing illumination.

"You're looking for me," Akira said, matter-of-factly, as she emerged from the darkness of the trees ahead of him. Step by step, the moonlight revealed more of her body until her face, glowing against the night appeared within inches of his.

"I'm supposed to find you, right?" he asked. "Why else are you coming to me unless we're supposed to be together?"

She leaned in so closely he could feel her breath tickling his lips. "You're not happy with the way things are?"

"I love the way things are," he said, "but I have to wake up and endure the hours of my day without you. That's not an easy thing to do."

She kissed him in the way that had caused him to surrender hundreds of times to her. Yielding completely, he made love to her, as the night embraced them like a comforter on a winter day.

Before he could climax, she whispered into his ear, "Don't look for me in the real world. Love me here. I will always be here for you."

"But…"

And as his entire dream world gave way and dissipated into nothingness, he found himself alone in his darkened loft, unable to make out anything, save the light of the street lamps touching the many acrylic faces along the wall.

❧

THE FOLLOWING MONDAY night Apollo found himself once again surrounded by images of Akira, though these were the paintings Jackson Parks had rendered for his debut one-man show. Cesar floated around like a bumblebee dropping onto the pistils of various conversations throughout the gallery. Jackson stood about glad-handing anyone who showed interest in his work. Apollo, meanwhile, stood off to the side, a small glass of wine in hand, unable to look away from Akira's face.

It seemed such a cruel trick of fate that he would be haunted and taunted by this woman in his dreams, but even more, he felt that she had stunted him in some small way when she told him not to seek her out in the real world. Why not? He could only imagine.

He was aware of the clichéd adage that reality could never truly live up to what was manifested in a dream, but he found that difficult to accept. It made absolutely no sense to him that this woman would be a real person and he not make any effort whatsoever to seek her out. He could not count the number of times Akira had come to him. His obsession with her had translated into his inability to find satisfaction with anyone in the real world. Anita had sensed this, but she hadn't been the only one. There had been other women who felt they didn't have his complete and undivided attention. The "art as mistress" concept was too heavy for most people, but this thing with Akira pushed far beyond that.

So Apollo continued to stare at each canvas around him, feeling himself to be the focus of the eyes staring back from the canvases. He was so locked into Akira's many gazes that he failed to hear Jackson come up behind him.

"Apollo, my man," he said, dapping Apollo.

"Jack, this is a great turnout!"

"Yeah. I sold five pieces already and just got a card from this art agent who wants to meet with me later this week."

"Congratulations! That's great news!" Apollo surprised himself with the authenticity of his comment. He was not one to have many friends, but Jackson was a good guy, definitely deserving of the blessings headed his way.

"Cesar and I are headed out afterwards to celebrate. If you're free, you can join us."

"Sure," he responded. He hadn't been out in who knows how long, but he knew he was overdue for just hanging out with people who loved art as much as he and who were pushing the movement forward for other Black artists.

"Well, stick around—and if you're inclined to, buy a piece," Jackson said, laughing again at his own joke.

"You know what?" Apollo said. "I'll take this one here." He pointed to the one he had been fixating on at the far end of the wall.

"I'll make sure Cesar gives you the artist rate," Jackson said, again dapping Apollo. "Thanks for looking out for a brotha."

"No problem."

As Jackson walked away, Apollo turned to face the painting he was acquiring. In his heart, he felt it was the best of the lot, but he knew that collectors tended to obsess over many of the things that were not of interest to actual artists.

He also knew, as he looked at the familiar face staring back at him from the canvas, he would begin, in earnest, seeking out the woman who had manifested herself to two different artists in two very different ways.

✺

THE BAR WAS one of those upscale spots frequented by those who constituted the "in" crowd, the kind of place where everyone ordered liquor from the top shelf and made sure to position themselves throughout the place to see and be seen by those who mattered in whatever industry that converged there for the evening. This evening the place was populated by artists of various types: singers, stage and film actors, and artists, not unlike Apollo and Jackson. Cesar had called ahead to reserve a booth for them, and when they arrived, it seemed as though everything in The City that night was being celebrated. It was the kind of place Apollo generally abhorred, but it was Jackson's night, and he wanted to support his new friend as best he could.

"That was a pretty strong opening night," Cesar said, his smile covering half of his face.

"Yeah," Jackson responded, Cesar's smile apparently bearing its on contagion. "I don't know what I had expected initially, but it wasn't that."

Apollo felt compelled to add his two cents. "That was a hell of a show." The words were honest, but largely unnecessary. The proof of the night's success had been the pieces Jackson had sold and that he had lined up a meeting with an art agent.

"I'm just trying to take it all in," Jackson said.

Cesar nodded his head. "The critics looked like they were feeling you, too, but you can never be a hundred percent with that group. Either way, I think it was good for getting your name out there. Hopefully the rest of the week will be just as strong."

As Apollo listened, a thought slowly emerged. He leaned forward and faced Jackson. "Outside of the piece I bought from you, how many of the pieces that you sold were of Akira?"

Jackson considered this for a moment and then responded with a bit of surprise. "All of them."

"All of them," Apollo repeated. He then turned to face Cesar. "I can't do a show where I'm using the exact same model as Jack. My work would seem entirely derivative. I've gotta change out my pieces."

Jackson jumped in. "Come on, Apollo. We talked about this."

"I know. But I can't go through with it. I've got to change it up."

"At least keep the one of her in the hotel. That piece is amazing."

Apollo suddenly felt like all of the paintings were too

personal to display after all. He needed to get back to his studio and sort out his thoughts.

"At least sleep on it," Cesar said. "You've got some really good pieces. The Pre-Raphaelites didn't have a problem with painting the same model. I think you're overthinking this thing just a little."

Apollo shook his head. "I appreciate what you two are trying to do, but you just don't get it. She wasn't a model to me. She was more than that, and, honestly, I think that makes my paintings of her too personal for an exhibition. I need to revisit some of my other pieces."

"You only get one chance to make a first impression," Cesar said. "Put your best foot forward and use your best work. I believe that if you were totally serious with yourself, you'd use your most recent paintings. Your work looks and feels very inspired. You can't fake or force that."

Apollo sat quietly for a moment, considering this. When he realized that his existential moment was draining energy from the celebration, he said, "Hey, I'll figure it out. But, Jack, tell me about this agent. You're moving on up like George Jefferson."

Jackson laughed and Cesar joined in.

As they continued to talk over drinks, Apollo never mentioned Akira again, but she was never far away from his thoughts.

◦✦◦

ONCE HE STEPPED outside the bar, Apollo froze in his tracks, stunned by the sight of someone roughly two blocks down the street on the opposite side. Not believing his eyes, he tried to carefully navigate to the other side of the street, before racing down the sidewalk. By the time he reached the end of the first block, he could no longer see her. She had disappeared into the throng of night activity.

Apollo stood in the same spot for several minutes wondering if what he had seen was Akira or if his mind was just so fixated on her image that he was seeing her in virtually everything he did. He walked a bit farther, checking down side streets, and even wandered into several bars scattered along the next few blocks, but there were no traces of anyone who resembled Akira. He shrugged his shoulders, but his heart continued to race as he walked back to his loft.

He reached home a little after midnight, put on *Maxwell's Urban Hang Suite*, and stared at the paintings lining his wall. Cesar was right. The pictures of Akira were by far the best paintings he had, but he was no longer convinced he should use them. Because both he and Jackson painted in a hyper-realistic way, there wasn't much in the way of distinguishing the artwork to the casual observer. Yes, he could tell his own brush strokes, but the fact that both he and Jackson used acrylics made the differentiation far subtler. To a lot of the people who were in attendance tonight, it would appear as if Apollo's exhibit was just part two of Jackson's exhibit. He would definitely need to go back to his original plans for the show.

Then he noticed the painting of the hotel with the solitary visible face in the painting being that of Akira. He might use that one, he figured, but he couldn't afford to use the others.

He would sleep on it, just like Cesar had suggested, but as he turned off the lights and lay down in his bed, the image of the painting, the image of what he thought he had seen on the sidewalk, and the image of Akira from his dreams merged into a single entity that welcomed him into the surrealistic dream world he had come to cherish.

No sooner than he closed his eyes, he was in a mansion—not quite a Buckingham Palace or Biltmore Estate—more like a large old, but livable home. As he walked into the main room off from the foyer, he noticed stairs that descended into the basement. With the sunlight streaming into the house, he headed downstairs.

There were no halls in the basement, only consecutive rooms, like five game rooms lined up back to back to back to back to back. Once he reached the end of the last room, he noticed a thin, swirling staircase. Something told him to climb it, so he did.

As he went up the stairs, he noticed that he was walking past the main floor and that there was absolutely no way to access that floor from the stairwell. The stairs delivered him to the third floor of the house. It was as if the only way to reach that new hall of rooms was to go through the basement to get to them.

He opened a door to the closest room and was surprised to see it decorated in such an intimate and personal way. It didn't look like it was designed for a queen; it looked like it was designed for a couple who actually used the bedroom to sleep in and not showcase to company. He walked over to the window, once again taking in the sunlight that had held him when he first entered the house.

"Hey, you," he could hear Akira's voice say behind him. "Another room for us to share."

"Yes. I really want you."

"But you keep looking for me. You have to stop that."

"Or what?" he said, playfully.

"Or you'll lose me."

This time Apollo's face stiffened. "How can I lose you? Regardless of what happens, we will always have this."

Akira lowered her head. "You just don't get it, do you?"

"What's there to get? This is *my* dream, and I want you here."

Akira walked over to him and placed a gentle kiss upon his lips. "Your dreams belong to you, Apollo. I don't."

The daylight turned to night as Apollo found himself, eyes wide open, staring at the ceiling of his loft. He looked around, but with each movement of his body, he realized he was no longer asleep. He tried to go back to sleep, and after an hour or so of struggling, he eventually did, but this time he did not dream.

৩৫৩

THE PHONE WOKE Apollo from his sleep. He had forgotten to turn off the ringer, so the sound of Björk's "I Miss You" blasted through the speakers of his smart phone, jolting him. He reached for it blindly not fully aware of the time of day.

"Hello?" he said, clearing his voice. It was the first time he had used it in lord knows how long. He glanced at his watch and quickly deduced that it was a quarter to noon.

"Hey, Apollo, this is Jack."

"What's up?" he responded, sitting up on the edge of his bed, trying to clear his head.

"I hope you don't mind that Cesar gave me your number."

"Nah. That's cool. What's up?"

"I got some info on Akira and wanted to share it with you."

"Oh shit!" Apollo jumped to his feet, his head as clear as Caribbean water. "What did you find out?" He could hardly believe his good fortune, and he had trouble suppressing his excitement.

"So, check this out. One of my boys who used to sit in on some of the art classes back in the day told me that the girl's name was Akira Beetz. He always wrote down everything he could about the people who posed for us. I know it's not much, but it's a last name. I figure that might help out a little with your search."

Apollo's smile was now making his face ache. "This is perfect. Thanks, Jack. I owe you one."

"No problem."

"At least I can treat you to lunch somewhere in the neighborhood."

Jack laughed. "I'm not turning down free food, but it would have to be after I get back from France. I'll be leaving once the exhibition wraps up. Got a fellowship."

"Wow! Congrats. Yeah, we can definitely connect when you get back."

"A'ight. Be easy, man. Peace," Jackson said, hanging up.

Apollo ran over to his laptop and sat down in the swivel cushioned office chair that often had to be pumped up repeatedly to keep its height. Entering the name Akira Beetz into the search engine didn't bring up anything familiar, definitely not his muse. But now he was determined, so he decided to do a white pages search of the surname Beetz for Atlanta, hoping like hell that she lived in the city and not one of the many suburbs that would take much longer to scan.

Ten names came up for Beetz, which was incredibly refreshing. Part of him expected that, although the name was not particularly common, in a large city like Atlanta, it could very well be the surname for a hundred people. He quickly grabbed his phone and started calling names on the list.

The first three numbers went straight to voicemail with the default recording of a voice reading back the number and providing no additional information. The fourth number was for an elderly man named Dolf Beetz. Another strike out. He continued down the list, once again getting useless voicemail prompts. When he called the penultimate name on the list, Gertrude Beetz, the phone picked up.

For a moment there was silence, so Apollo said, "Hello?"

There was the sound of someone juggling the phone for a

moment. Then the voice came through. "Hello?" It was the voice of a woman who sounded not unlike his own mother, that Southern flavor of a woman who belonged to a certain generation of Black mothers.

"Hi. My name is Apollo, and I'm trying to find someone by the name of Akira Beetz."

"Who is this?" the woman asked.

"Apollo," he responded, repeating himself.

"Like the Greek god? Or the boxer?"

He smiled. "The boxer, ma'am."

"Now who do you want?"

"Akira?" he repeated.

"Akira?"

Then another voice from the background emerged. "Momma, that's the name Angie used to use."

Angie. So that was her real name. Angie Beetz, Apollo thought. He had finally found her!

"You calling for Angie?"

Apollo nodded furiously, before realizing that the woman on the other end of the phone could not see him. "Yes, ma'am."

There was a long pause. "Baby," the woman started, "Angie passed away last year."

Stunned and not ready to concede defeat, Apollo added, "The Akira I'm looking for used to be an art model."

"Yep. That's Angie. My angel."

Apollo felt as if someone had yanked the chair out from beneath him. "Ma'am, can I ask you one question? If it's not too much, could you tell me what happened?"

"There was this incident at a party in the West End, and she got shot by someone who was aiming at someone else."

"Well, I'm very sorry for your loss," Apollo said, blinking through the water clouding his vision.

"Thank you, baby. You take care of yourself, too, ya hear?"

"Yes, ma'am."

After he hung up his phone, he sat in the chair and swiveled it toward the paintings along the wall. He still couldn't understand why he was crying. He had never met this woman in real life or held a conversation with her. Up until a minute ago he had not even known her name, yet he had fallen in love with her in his dreams. She was the embodiment of perfection, the common denominator in all that was good in his life. It was his unwavering desire to believe in her existence that cramped his entire romantic life. He was not fit for anyone, as long as Akira (or Angie) was somewhere out there.

But she had warned him not to seek her in the real world. Why hadn't he listened to her? Life wasn't intended to be lived like those poor souls sleeping their lives away in *Inception*. He needed for her to be real, and like some kind of twisted "monkey's paw" wish, she had been real, but she was no longer alive. Staring at paintings of her, Apollo couldn't imagine that beautiful, angelic face somewhere decomposing in the earth. A stray bullet, too. Something that might have been avoided by a slight alteration in time or movement, the kind of thing that people have wished to have time machines to fix.

The woman whose face rested before him was no more, and he had willingly walked into that knowledge, against her wishes.

Once his eyes dried, he realized this situation only placed him back where he had been initially, where she had only existed in his dreams. He would have to be satisfied with that from here forward, he reasoned. At least he would still have her in a way that made sense to him, if it didn't make sense to anyone else.

⚜

THAT NIGHT when Apollo went to sleep, he did not dream of Akira. He tried repeatedly over the next two days to dream of her, but she was gone. It was as if her pleads to him in that last dream were a warning that he would lose her altogether if he knew the truth about her. The realization he may have lost her twice caused him to draw deeply into himself, and he turned his loft into a dark chrysalis, pulling down the blinds to block out all of the light that once flooded his studio. The darkness washed over everything, and he found himself drifting in and out of dreamless consciousness, unaware of what time of day it was.

Finally, after a bland and restless nap (he couldn't tell anymore what were naps versus actual sleep), he found himself hungry. With his refrigerator empty of everything except three partially filled water bottles, he tossed on a t-shirt, a pair of sweatpants, and some gym shoes. Only when he reached the front door did he know what time of day it was. It looked like late afternoon.

He headed two blocks down to a deli known for its corned beef sandwiches. It was the closest thing to the smoked meat sandwiches he'd fallen in love with in Montreal the summer before. Suddenly, he felt he could eat a hundred of them. He walked into the deli and bought three of them, several bags of chips, and several cans of soda. He planned to take everything back to the loft and eat over the next few days so he wouldn't have to leave his place again for a while.

As he waited for his food, he stared through the front window at the surrounding neighborhood. When he had first arrived in The City five years earlier, he'd struggled to contain his excitement at not only having moved there, but also having found an affordable spot in the art district. The neighborhood wasn't gentrified (yet), like other cities of the same ilk. As a result, everything was still old school Mom & Pop-centered, sans kale smoothies or vegan hot dogs. There was an earthy element to everything, the kind of place where it could be beautiful-beautiful one minute and beautiful-ugly the next—but there was always a beauty there. Apollo couldn't imagine living anywhere else in the world.

Then he saw the bright face of a woman walking away from his sightline across the street. Her face caused his heart to beat heavily in his chest. It looked like Akira, but her Afro was gone. Her hair was cut into a low, natural style. He quickly left the store and ran in her direction, but by the time he got across the street, he could no longer see her. He scanned the street again, and then it dawned on him. This was her way of saying goodbye to him now that he knew she was dead. Something in his soul smiled at this.

He returned to the deli and picked up his food. When he made it back to his loft, he let the blinds up.

The darkness was still there, but he knew at some point he had to let the light back in.

❧

APOLLO CONSIDERED SPEAKING with Cesar about canceling the show, but then his saner thoughts prevailed. For art to be his future, he would need to follow through with everything he set out to do. Maybe what had happened for Jackson could happen for him, too. He definitely needed to remain open to all opportunities and possibilities.

His journey to this one-man show had not been without its struggles. Before he moved to The City to pursue his art, he had been an art major whose longest job had been a stint working in a gas station convenience store, praying like hell every night he didn't get robbed on the job. During the daytime, he served as an art teacher for the local community center in his town, a job that paid via a quarterly honorarium, far beneath minimum wage.

His aunt Alice, who was a college professor on the upper east coast, became aware of the job at Barnes Design College through an academic employment listserve, helped Apollo shape his curriculum vitae to fit the qualifications, and even served as a reference for him. It was the move that forever transformed his life and how he viewed his art. In just five years he had made a number of connections in the art community and had finally made his way to a one-man show. With his background, he was never guaranteed any of these opportunities, so he had to keep placing one foot in front of the other to keep up the momentum.

Akira had been the only hiccup since he arrived in The City. Now he was determined to move on with his life, with his art.

With his show coming up in another six days, he began selecting his pieces, one by one. Of his new paintings he included only the hotel painting. His other pieces were various images that captured everything from City life to elements of his hometown in Jackson, Tennessee. It wasn't that the other pieces were bad— after all, Cesar had approached him about the exhibition based on the strength of those pieces—it was just that there was a kind of fever, some indescribably, but clearly palpable, passion that danced off the canvases of those paintings of Akira.

On a small level the paintings had a haunting effect on him. That Angie had been dead the entire time he had been dreaming of her made him feel uneasy. Even now, with this knowledge, she had still not returned to his dreams. The whole experience spooked him, as if his psyche had been intruded upon in some supernatural way. It had been love, though, right? It wasn't like he feared her in his dreams; in fact, it was very much the opposite. This ambivalence tore at him when he looked at the paintings. Once he decided to only include the hotel, he covered the others with white sheets so he did not have to confront her image any more than he had to. Maybe then he could recover from all he had experienced.

Once he organized all of his artwork for the show, he called Cesar to come over and take a look at everything. He wanted to make sure the pieces worked together as a whole. Cesar's gallery was very small and informal, but Cesar took pride in making sure his exhibitions were professionally presented. He, too, aspired to higher rungs on the art business ladder.

"Well, well, well," Cesar said, moving back and forth between the pieces. He walked around the loft several times, taking in the artwork at various angles. "I don't know."

"What's wrong?" Apollo asked.

"I don't know. It just feels inconsistent."

"How so?"

"It's the hotel piece that concerns me."

"So you want me to remove it?"

Cesar shook his head slowly and indecisively. "That's the thing. It's your best piece. If we take it out, then people won't know just how good you are. If we keep it in, it throws off the flow of all the other pieces you have." Cesar glanced around the room again. "The paintings under the sheets over there, are those the other paintings of the girl?"

"Yes."

Cesar nodded. Apollo had already explained what had happened to Akira, so Cesar didn't ask any further questions about it.

"You want me to use the other pictures of Akira," Apollo said matter-of-factly.

Cesar paused before answering. "I just want you to put on the best show you can."

Apollo pulled up his office chair and sat down. His mother had once told him that no person should make long-term decisions off of short-term emotions. "Okay. Let's do it," he said. "Let's use all of the new paintings."

"You sure?" Cesar asked.

"Nope. But let's do it anyway."

☙❧

CESAR CALLED ONCE the movers had gotten the pieces into the gallery. Apollo headed right over.

As he and Cesar carefully hung the pieces in the arrangement they'd sketched out at the loft, Apollo secretly wished his parents could have attended the opening. His father's work in Dubai meant that his parents were hardly ever in the United States. He would send them a care package with photographs when everything was over, though.

Once all of the pieces had been hung, both he and Cesar stood back smiling.

"This is really something," Cesar said.

"You don't think people will think my show looks too much like Jackson's?"

"I'm not a mind reader, but I think your take on Akira, uh Angie, is very different than Jack's."

Apollo nodded. He figured as much, but as an artist it was sometimes difficult to articulate gut feelings about art.

Cesar continued. "Jack paints her as a model. You do something very different with her. It feels almost like you *deify* her."

Apollo hadn't expected that. He had never considered that at all, but now that he had heard the words, they seemed strangely apt. "I hope that's a good thing," he said.

"It's art of the highest kind, my brother," Cesar said, patting him on the back.

"Thanks."

"So come Monday night, we're gonna set this thing out like nobody's business. A'ight?"

A smile slowly spread across Apollo's face. "Yeah. Let's do this."

"Oh, before I forget, Jack left something here for you before he headed out to Paris."

Cesar disappeared into the back of the gallery and returned with the painting Apollo had committed to purchasing from Jackson.

"Wow, I almost forgot about it, with all that's been going on."

"No problem."

"You accept credit cards right?"

"You know I do—but Jack and I agreed you should have this one free of charge, especially with all you've been going through lately."

Apollo lowered his head, humbled by the gesture. "I have to pay for it. That's how we make a living as artists."

"He refuses to take any money from you," Cesar said.

"Well, what about your commission?"

"I'm about to make plenty of commissions off of the pieces in here right now."

Apollo smiled. "Thanks, Cesar. I mean it. Thanks for everything."

"Hey, it's all right. Just keep painting. Keep your head up. And on Monday, we're gonna show these people what you're all about."

"Will do."

※

ALTHOUGH APOLLO ARRIVED at the gallery early on Monday night to acclimate himself to the environment, his nerves were still totally frayed when people began walking through the door. He had to step out back several times to get some air and settle himself down. At that moment, he wished he could talk to Jackson for a few minutes, maybe get some tips on how to manage his nerves.

Then his phone rang. He glanced at the caller ID and saw that it was his father.

"Andy, how's it going?"

"Hey, Dad, I'm all over the place."

"Your mom told me that we should call you before the show starts because you were always the person who got pretty anxious about public attention."

"Tell him we love him," Apollo could hear his mother saying in the background.

"I love you guys, too."

"Andy, let's do the thing that Dr. Sherman used to have you do."

Apollo could feel his heart rate starting to slow down a little. "Okay."

"I'm handing the phone to your mother," his father said.

"Okay, baby. It's me. I want you to close your eyes, okay? We're gonna breathe really deeply and when we do, we're going to count down slowly from ten. You ready?"

"Yes, Mom."

As he breathed deeply and his mother counted, he felt his pulse slow down. His urge to jump outside of his body and run away began to diminish in very small increments. By the time she had done the exercise for about a minute, Apollo's heart rate was just slightly above what it would have been had he been sitting at rest. He could definitely manage his nerves now.

"You good, son?" his father said.

"Yes. Thank you so much! I'm actually surprised to hear from you and Mom."

"We had it marked on our phone's calendar to call you. We'll be back in the States in December. We can celebrate properly then."

"Sure thing."

"Now go in there and show them what you're about," his mother said.

"Ditto on what your mother said," his father added.

"I love you guys."

"We love you, too," his parents responded.

Once he had hung up his phone, he smoothed out his blazer and rubbed his hands through his hair. Now he was ready.

He entered the backdoor of the gallery and found his way around to the main area, where people had already started pouring in.

He stared in disbelief. They were there to see *his* work. This was really happening.

He scanned the crowd for Cesar and when he spotted him, he completely submerged himself into his identity as Apollo and slowly stepped forward to work the room.

۞

ROUGHLY AN HOUR after the show had begun, Apollo noticed her. She was standing in the corner staring at one of the portraits he had re-imagined from his dream. Her hair was short, very closely cropped in a low fade, the top wavy and shorter than his own. But the face was unmistakable. It was Akira.

Not totally sure he was actually seeing what he believed he was seeing, he approached her cautiously, but with an accelerated step, just in case she disappeared as she had done those other two times.

When he reached her, she was standing there, her eyes fixed on the painting. He could smell the scent of her fruit-infused lotion. This was a real person, not an illusion.

"Hi," he said, saddling up next to her as nonchalantly as he could manage over his thunderously pounding heart.

"Hi," she responded.

Not knowing what else to say, he asked, "What do you think?" It seemed like the kind of question one might ask another in an art gallery.

"This is crazy realistic!" she said, turning her head to the side. "The funny thing is that I don't even remember posing for this. One of my girlfriends told me she had seen a picture of me in here a few weeks ago, so I figured I'd come by to see it. I had no idea that I was the focus of the entire exhibit! She didn't tell me that part."

Apollo stared at her, unable to put together two coherent words. He knew he didn't want to start with the fact that she was referencing Jackson's paintings and not his own. And the idea of telling her about the dreams just seemed *way* over the top, given that he was still adjusting to the fact that she was standing here. Was she a ghost?

"But your question was what did I think of the painting. It's pretty incredible."

He tried not to stare at her too hard for fear of making her feel uneasy.

"Well, thank you," he finally mustered, figuring he would at least let her know he was the artist of the portrait. "I'm Apollo."

"Oh, so these are yours then?" she responded.

"Yes," he said, bashful for the first time in years. "And your name?" he asked, extending his hand. He really wanted to touch her, just to make sure she was real.

When her hand grasped his and he felt the warmth of her flesh pressed against his, he nearly passed out. He missed her name and quickly asked her to repeat it.

"Dani."

"Dani," he repeated. She had already admitted to being the woman in the paintings, so this latest revelation baffled him.

"Well, actually my name is Tupelo. Tupelo Daniels. But I just think Tupelo is a funny name for a girl. My grandmother grew up there, so my mom thought it would be a cool name for me. I prefer people to call me Dani."

He nodded, trying to conceal his confusion. "Yeah, Apollo's not my government name either."

"If you don't mind, can I ask you what your real name is?"

"Sure. It's Andrew Fields."

"That's pretty different. Sounds like a park in The City."

"Yeah, I guess." He smiled. "I picked up the nickname 'Apollo' from one of my white classmates growing up because he said I reminded him of Apollo Creed. Creed was dope, but I don't think that's what this kid was getting at. To him, Apollo was just Black. To me, Apollo was a smart, charismatic guy who happened to be the heavyweight champion of the world."

"I feel you on that."

He had a million questions sitting on the edge of his tongue, and he felt like he could talk to her for hours, but he didn't want to scare her off. "Are you going to be around for a little bit longer?" he asked.

"Sure."

Her response made him smile. "I'd love to talk with you some more, maybe grab a drink when things wrap up here?"

"That's cool."

He hated the idea of walking away from her, but he knew he had to make the rounds. Plus, he wanted to take a moment to let the reality of what was happening seep in.

He glanced back at her and was surprised to see her looking at him—no, checking him out. It was beyond any dream he could have fathomed.

Akira—Dani was not only alive. She was here.

He didn't know how the woman on the phone had gotten so many facts about Dani wrong, but he hoped he could put all of that madness to rest when he got to know the literal woman of his dreams.

IT HADN'T BEEN easy turning down Cesar's request for drinks to celebrate the opening of the show, but he had no choice but to take a rain check. After Apollo explained to him what was happening, Cesar smiled and told him to go forth and have fun.

Apollo still couldn't believe Dani had agreed to have drinks with him. He was so full of questions that if she so much as touched him, a steady stream of them would have leaped from his lips.

After taking seats at a booth in the back of a relatively small bar a few blocks from the gallery, Dani said, "I'm still floored that I'm the focus of your entire collection."

"Well, those were the best pieces."

She laughed and shook her head. "I only posed one time and it inspired an entire show."

"One time?" Apollo had been led to believe that she had been a regular art model.

"Yeah. My girl was the real model. She did them all the time." Dani took a sip of her drink. "I was in between jobs and begged to model that one time so I could cover my phone bill. She was kind enough to let me go in her place, so I just used her name for the session since it was already listed on the paperwork that way."

"What was your friend's name?" Apollo asked.

"Angie. But she preferred for people to call her Akira."

He slowly nodded his head as the pieces of the puzzle began to assemble themselves before his eyes. Knowing the answer to his next question, he still plowed ahead. "And does Angie still model?"

Dani lowered her head and shook it solemnly. "She passed away." She took a long pause and then had another sip of her drink. "I think after Angie was killed, I decided to leave Atlanta. I took a job in DC and came up here to check out some opportunities when things didn't work out down there."

Apollo nodded. Hearing all of this was an incredible relief. He couldn't believe his good fortune.

"So what type of work do you do?"

"I'm a chef."

He hadn't expected her to say those words, but he immediately grew intrigued. "A chef?"

"Yes. I've always enjoyed cooking, so after teaching first grade for three years, I went to culinary school. I've been doing it for the past four years. I love it."

"Well, maybe one day I can taste your food," Apollo responded. It wasn't a very original line, but it was honest nonetheless.

As the night went on and their conversation relaxed with the mental lubrication afforded them by the alcohol, he decided to come clean with her.

"The artist who painted you at your sitting was actually another artist named Jackson. He had a show at that gallery two weeks ago. That's the one your friend must have seen."

"I don't understand," Dani said.

"Well, I painted all of my portraits of you because I dreamed of you. Honestly, I didn't even know you were real until I saw Jackson's paintings a few weeks back and he mentioned you were a model in Atlanta."

She tilted her head quizzically, still unable to make sense of what he was saying.

"I don't know how it happened, but I kept dreaming about you and just decided to paint you. I had never seen you before anywhere, had never even seen Jackson's paintings. My paintings came straight from my dreams."

Dani was quiet for a moment. Then she began laughing heartily at the table. "This sounds like a Meshell Ndegeocello song. The world has made me the woman of your dreams!"

"I guess so," Apollo responded, laughing along with her uneasily.

She stopped laughing and took another sip of what remained in her glass. "I'm literally the woman of your dreams." She said this plainly, as if she were reading him the time from a wristwatch.

He nodded slowly.

"Well, I have to say I'm flattered—and just a little bit weirded out."

"Sorry to make you feel uncomfortable."

"Don't say that," she responded.

"What?"

"That you're sorry. Because you aren't. You meant to tell me that, so don't apologize."

"Okay," he said, curious to see what direction the conversation would take from that point forward.

"So I guess I should ask you what I do in these dreams of yours."

"Well, it's like we're together."

"So what do I do? Do I suck you off or something?"

Her brashness confused him and accelerated his thoughts so rapidly he could scarcely mesh his dreams with what was happening at that exact moment in the bar.

"At times we're intimate," he finally responded.

"Intimate?"

"Yes."

"So you fuck me in your dreams?"

Apollo didn't know if this was the alcohol talking or what, but he felt the conversation had jumped the rails. It no longer felt like they were in the middle of a romantic evening. It felt much more *carnal* than that.

"Dreams are dreams. I'm just trying to get to know the person who is in front of me right now."

"But dreams are more than dreams, clearly," she responded. "You don't paint all of those pictures with it just being something that's trivial."

He shrugged his shoulders, not knowing what to say.

"One thing about working in a kitchen is that you don't sugar-coat things. You just come right out with it. We are direct. If my being this direct is off-putting, just let me know."

"No. You're fine."

For a moment they sat in silence, Dani staring at him, sizing him up. He felt himself incredibly intimidated by her, but he fought not to show it.

"You're pretty handsome," she finally said.

"Thank you. And you're very beautiful."

"So, in keeping with my mantra of being direct, I have to ask you this. Do you want to sleep with me?"

It was in no way what he had imagined, but then his dreams didn't consist of some drawn out process of wooing her for her affections. Come to think of it, they kind of came to each other almost immediately.

"Yes."

"See. That wasn't so hard."

"I guess not."

"Do you live near here?"

"Just a few blocks away."

"Well, let's leave then."

The walk back to his loft was filled with random observations, as if they had not just agreed to have sex. Dani remarked about a broken down car with a Lyft sticker in the back, her favorite coffee beans, and the fact that she could prepare an egg over a hundred ways but could never bring herself to eat one. "People will eat anything," she said, laughing at her own joke.

Once they reached the loft, he stared at her with only the light of the street lamps illuminating her. She was beautiful, and ironically the only place her face existed in the loft at that moment was as a part of her body, not some canvas lining the wall.

She pulled him closer and kissed him gently. The taste of rum coated her lips, and he worried that she might not know what she was doing. He didn't want to be with her like this, but she beat him to it.

"I just want to chill tonight. Is that cool?"

"Sure," he said, relieved. He wanted their first time being intimate to be one that they both remembered and entered into with clear heads.

He lay on his bed and she snuggled against him, the two of them spooning in their clothes, as the sounds of The City from outside the windows moved around them like a familiar soundtrack.

❧

DURING THE MIDDLE of the night, he could feel her hands against his chest, her kisses moving passionately up and down his neck. Unsure of whether or not he was awake, he pulled her closer out of familiarity. Barely able to see the other's body, they disrobed each other until their warm flesh was pressed together.

She didn't say anything, and neither did he.

He entered her, and she gasped as she held him in her arms. It was like a dream, but also very different. He could still smell traces of their drinks from earlier, but their actions were very deliberate and sober.

They continued, changing positions, pausing to taste the other, desperate to please the other until they collectively climaxed.

Afterwards, they lay side-by-side, breathless.

When she finally spoke, he realized that this was the real thing. "I need to use the bathroom."

"Sure. It's right down there," he said, angling her towards the dark corner of the loft.

"Well, that isn't spooky at all," she said, laughing.

"I could join you," he offered.

"All right."

Using the glow of the streetlights, he escorted her to the bathroom and started the shower. They stood under the warm water, content to wash each other in the darkness of the room. His fingers traced her body through soapy suds, and she placed her hands along the sides of his face, kissing him periodically as he touched her.

Once they finished their shower, they returned to the bed and covered themselves in the thin sheet resting on top of the mattress. They resumed their spooning, and this time they slept until the night gave way to the light of morning.

⊙⊱⊙

HE AWOKE to Dani's voice, but it was not directed at him.

"Thank you," she said, her face animated. "I can fly out tomorrow."

When she hung up the phone, he walked over to the desk where she was seated and kissed her forehead. She tugged at his loose boxers, awakening his erection.

"I see you're up and you're *up*," she said, laughing.

He smiled, barely noticing how tightly the fabric pulled at his hips. He wanted her—of course—but her words were still ringing in his ears. "Fly out *tomorrow*?"

"Yeah. I have a job lined up in San Jose."

He felt, for a moment, as if he could not understand the language she was speaking. "San Jose. What job?"

"It's a sous chef position with a start-up out there. Mediter-ranean food. High end."

He pulled up one of the spare chairs he had lining that side of the loft. "You're literally leaving tomorrow?"

"Yeah. I was only passing through here. I had feelers out here, San Jose, and Dallas. I'm pretty sure my friend wants her sofa back, too." At this, she laughed, again.

What was up with all of this laughing? She hadn't been like that in his dreams. What was so damn funny all the time?

He knew that his anger didn't stem from her laughter, though. He had been searching for her, had found her, and was now about to lose her, unless he could say something to stop her from leaving.

"Can't you stay here? I'm sure there are opportunities in The City. Eight million people and all."

"This is a cool place, don't get me wrong, but I like the West Coast vibe a lot more."

Feeling a bit more desperate than he expected, he said, "But we just met. Well, I can schedule to fly out to see you and maybe we can meet halfway. What's halfway between the East Coast and the West Coast?"

Dani stared at him, but this time she was not smiling. "Apollo, I can't do this."

"Do what? The distance? Hell, I can look for a job out there."

"You don't even know me."

"But I want to."

She reached for his hand and held it in hers. "But I don't want anything serious. I like you. We had a great time, but I don't make decisions based off emotions."

That line sounded mighty familiar, Apollo thought.

"I dreamed of you. Surely that means something, right?"

"I don't know. It allowed you to paint portraits that will help your career."

He bristled at this. "It's not about the art to me. It's about *you*."

Dani shrugged her shoulders. "You just met me last night. This can't be about me. This is about your idea of me."

"I just want to get to know you better. Last night was good. We really should give this thing a try."

"Apollo, I think you're missing the whole point. I just told you I got a job. A job! And the first thing you do is talk about how this affects *you*. I've been hustling my ass off this entire time. This is a big deal for me, but I guess that's besides the point, huh? A sista can't even get a congratulations up in this piece."

"It's not like that. I'm happy for you, really. Congratulations." He knew the words were just words at this point. He'd missed the chance to be authentic. He sighed, shaking his head. "I just want us to give this thing a chance."

"Frankly, I'm not even in an emotional space to deal with any kind of relationship right now. I'm still getting back on my feet. I just want to make this job work out."

Still wrestling with the notion that she would be gone the following day, he said, "In my dream you told me not to come looking for you in the real world. I guess you knew you would break my heart."

"Whoa. This is *way* too much for me," she said, rising from her chair and reaching for her purse. "You're weirding me out again."

"I'm sorry."

"And stop apologizing!" Now her temper was beginning to show. "I was going to ask if you wanted to spend the day hanging out before I left, but I don't think that's a good idea now. I should just leave."

He wanted her to stay, was prepared to beg her on bended knee, but he realized that he would only make her feel more uncomfortable. She wanted to leave. He wouldn't allow himself to hold her in his place against her wishes.

"Can I at least walk you to the door?"

"Okay."

They walked to the door in silence. When she faced him again, her face softened. "I enjoyed myself last night," she said.

She leaned in to kiss him, and as badly as he wanted to feel her lips again, he knew it didn't mean anything to her. He turned his head slightly, and she placed a simple kiss upon his cheek before leaving.

When she closed the door behind herself, Apollo returned to his bed and buried himself beneath the sweat-stained sheets. Her smell danced across the linen, and he closed his eyes.

He thought of the woman who had spent the night, then of the woman from his dreams. He wrestled to reconcile the two disparate images of her, and when he couldn't, he fell into an empty slumber.

⚘

WHEN APOLLO finally opened his eyes again, the room was dark, with only the light from the streets criss-crossing through his loft like bars holding him against his will. He desperately longed to call Dani, to apologize—no, show that he was willing to deal with the situation on her terms—but he did not have her phone number. In fact, he had no way of contacting her, as he did not know the name of the friend she was staying with. He had seen her twice in the neighborhood, so maybe she was nearby, but if she had wanted him to know where she was, she would have told him.

He could scarcely remember the feel of her body. That was one of the downfalls of being intimate in the early hours of the morning. He was unsure of whether his memories were real or remnants of a dream. Either way, she was no longer there, consciously or otherwise.

He walked over to the window and stared down into the streets. A few people, likely college students, ambled along to the bar on the next block up. Taxis swept slowly through intersections, searching for fares that were probably riding in the back of a Honda Accord, thanks to Uber and Lyft. He had loved the view from his loft, but now things felt empty, and he felt entirely alone.

He had been in The City for five years and had no real friends to speak of, only people who were associates from the art community. In fact, he had spent more time talking to Jackson and Cesar in the past three weeks than he had anyone in at least a year. Art was a solitary thing, and sometimes your life passed by in mid-stroke, the spring buried beneath a chartreuse, the previous winter beneath a cobalt, the fall before that beneath a burgundy.

But there was still the show, four more days for Apollo to capitalize on everything he hoped his art would achieve. He would go down to the gallery in the morning, talk to Cesar, and see where things stood. He hadn't met an art agent the previous night, but then he had spent much of his time as a bumblebee hovering over the rose that was Dani.

His heart ached and the emptiness, stemming from the past twenty-four hours, arrested him in a state of melancholy, but he knew life would have to continue on. He was thankful that all of the paintings of Dani had been moved from his loft to the gallery because he didn't know if he could take seeing her face at that moment.

He tried to imagine his life without having met her or dreamed her. What was so wrong with his life before? He and Anita had had a good thing, but he hadn't taken it all that seriously. He had never really given her a chance. After all, how could a real woman compete with an ideal in someone else's dreams? Even Dani, at her absolute best, would not have been able to live up to the perfection of his dreams. The problem wasn't Dani or Anita. It was Apollo himself.

He dragged himself back to his bed, the scent of her already fading into a memory of a memory. Then he closed his eyes once again.

☙❧

WHEN APOLLO AWOKE the following morning, he felt completely refreshed. Till that moment, he had not realized just how much sleeping he had been doing. When he thought about it briefly, he couldn't believe how much of his time he had deliberately chosen to spend unconscious. In this new clarity of mind, he could scarcely remember much about Dani or the long journey that had sent him on a quest to find her. Instead, he felt eager to tackle the day, unencumbered by any decisions he had made prior to that point.

The studio in his loft looked set up, ready for him. A blank white canvas rested on the easel, his older paintings lining the wall, as they had when he had originally planned to use them in his show.

So this was what a new beginning looked like, Apollo thought. It felt as if a weight had been removed from his chest. He would take things a day at a time and rebuild himself emotionally. He would continue painting. He would continue capturing the world through the unique lens of his paintbrush.

He tossed on a paint-splattered white t-shirt and a pair of jeans and walked across the warm hardwood floor to his easel.

Then his phone rang.

He scanned the room for his phone, finding it on the desk next to his computer.

He picked it up without looking at the caller ID. "Hello?"

"Hey, Apollo. This is Anita. We need to talk."

"Okay."

"Can I come over?"

"Come over? Aren't you in California?"

There was a pregnant pause.

"Who told you about California?"

"You did. You were leaving me for some film dude."

There was another pause, this one even longer. "I didn't tell you anything," she managed, uneasily.

Apollo stared at the blank canvas before him, then at the paintings along the wall, the exhibition he had planned before the Dani paintings.

No. It couldn't be, he thought.

"I'm here at home," he responded slowly. "We should definitely talk."

When he hung up the phone, he walked over to the blank canvas on the easel. The sun shown brightly through the loft, and while there was something familiar about the sky outside his window, there was the feeling of something new just beyond the glass pane.

He slowly picked up his pencil and allowed his hand to hover over the canvas. He thought about Dani's kiss and Jackson's paintings and his own muse-inspired exhibition and all the things he had experienced—or at least thought he had experienced. All of it had happened because of his decision to paint *her*.

Rotating the pencil in his hand and attempting to ignore the phantom pangs of his heart, Apollo leaned in closer to the canvas. As his brow furrowed, he realized he had no idea of what he would draw, yet, in the back of his mind, he knew exactly what he would not draw.

WHERE WOULD WE BE IF WE COULDN'T TWEET OUR THOUGHTS?

We were fond of Victor and Laura.

We didn't even mind that they frequently posted about their lives on social media; after all, we had attended their wedding and, in a way, felt we were just as invested in the success of their marriage as they were.

Their persistent posting was how we became aware that Victor and Laura were trying—unsuccessfully—to conceive. Laura documented everything in excruciating detail, often posting directly from her doctor's office.

We considered warning them about how much of their personal lives they posted online, but we relented. After all, what was a show without content?

When Laura vented her frustrations about their inability to have children, we felt her pain. When Victor tried to console her online (although they lived in the same house), we were touched by his love and support. Occasionally Laura would lash out at everyone—even Victor—and we wondered could their marriage survive the stress of it all.

So when Victor first posted that he and Laura were considering adopting, we were enthusiastic and supportive. We wanted a happy ending for them.

Then they became foster parents, and it was like the Victor and Laura Show had gotten a brand new season. Pictures of a new baby appeared six months later. More pictures of Victor and Laura, the model family with Baby Travis, posted in batches of ten. We knew everything that could be known about a six-month-old baby.

"Fingers crossed that we can adopt Travis," Laura posted several times each week, accompanied by another batch of pictures with Victor smiling while holding a soiled diaper above an open Diaper Genie.

They were happy with Travis, which is what made it so tragic when Travis's mother cleaned up long enough to petition for a restoration of her parental rights.

"It's not right!" Victor posted.

We all "liked" that post.

For a while after Victor and Laura lost Travis, they posted somber comments, reminiscing on every conceivable detail about Travis: his smell, his laugh, the sound of his snores.

We considered once again telling them to take their frustrations offline, to call us so we could properly console them.

"We're all family," they posted in response. And they continued posting.

After a while, things started to brighten a bit, and Laura posted that she and Victor were in talks with an adoption agency in Belize.

We "liked" that post, too.

Victor posted every conceivable detail, so by the time everything was approved and finalized and the two of them were on the plane headed to Belize, we were beside ourselves with joy for them.

As soon as the plane touched the runway in Belize, the social media posts rained in: pictures of the airport, the lush forests, the streets, the people. The pictures, in many ways, reminded us of their honeymoon pictures from Dominica. The difference here, though, was they would be returning with a new addition to their family.

Laura continued posting pictures even as they stood outside the adoption agency building. She sent a selfie of her cheesing with Victor looking on in the background, his eyes bright with expectation.

Then the posts stopped.

A day went by without any posts, and we all assumed that they were just overwhelmed with caring for a new life. Then another day passed.

Some of us posted messages of support on their page, asking them to check in and share the wonderful news about their new addition.

No response.

No response the next day either.

Finally Victor posted that he, Laura, and the baby were headed back to the States.

There were no posts for a week.

Then, out of nowhere, Laura posted one day, "Being a mother is a beautiful thing!"

And Victor posted, "I love my family!"

Gradually they resumed their posting, but this time the posts seemed generic—and none of the posts included pictures of the baby.

"Can we see the baby? Is it a boy or a girl?" some of us had asked.

An hour later, unusual by Victor and Laura's standards, a post went up on Laura's page in response to our inquiries: "Being a mother is a beautiful thing!"

Victor followed the comment with, "I love my family!"

This was the first sign to us that something wasn't altogether right with our favorite couple, so we waited a week and tried again, and when Victor and Laura gave the same cryptic responses, word for word, we decided to communicate via a direct group message among ourselves.

"What's going on with Victor and Laura?"

"They sound like robots? Maybe they were kidnapped in Belize, and someone is pretending to be them."

Once this comment was posted, the conspiracy gates really opened up.

"What if they went over there and couldn't adopt, so they're putting up a front?"

"Maybe there's something wrong with the baby, and they don't want us to see it."

"What if there is no baby and they are pretending to have a child?"

We didn't know what to think, and while we continued to press at Victor and Laura as diplomatically as we could, we still couldn't discern any responses to our questions.

Then one day, almost as if to stir the pot a bit, Victor posted a picture of Laura pushing a stroller at a park near their house. The baby was not visible, which did nothing to assuage our concerns.

There were selfies with a closed stroller. There were pictures of Victor covered in baby formula, as if putting together a bottle of milk was on par with baking a cake from scratch.

It wouldn't have been so unusual, except for the fact we had known so much about Travis. This time we didn't even know the sex of their baby, what the baby looked like, or even the baby's name. They had shared their lives online, but it was clear they weren't as open to sharing the life of their child in the same space.

We really should have let it go then, but we were far too invested in the Victor and Laura Show by then to turn away.

"At least let us host a baby shower for you," we posted.

After a day with no response, Laura responded, "Sure. We'd love that."

And that is how we all came to find ourselves in Victor and Laura's ranch house, just off the cul de sac of their subdivision. A closed baby carriage sat in front of us as we stood patiently waiting for them to remove the baby for us to see.

"She's sleeping," Victor said, and we nodded patiently, our gifts lining the kitchen and the dining room.

While we stood about idly chatting, Laura worked the room taking pictures of us and posting them to her social media accounts. #VicandLauraBabyShower.

Finally, one of us sneezed loudly, the kind of sneeze that sounded as if one's head was exploding into pieces and we all looked at the closed carriage, anticipating the wailing cry of a baby who was violently shaken from sleep.

There was dead silence. We looked at Victor and Laura. They shrugged.

Then one of us stated what we had all considered: "Is there a baby in there?"

"What do you mean?" Laura asked, her face filling with incredulity.

"We haven't heard a single sound or seen a single picture of a baby. We are your friends. It's time to stop this charade. Just admit that you don't have a baby. It's all right. We are still your friends. You don't have to pretend anymore."

Victor's voice rose in anger. "You don't believe we have a child. After all we have done for you ungrateful sons of bitches? Why would you host this baby shower for us if you didn't believe we had a baby? Are you making fun of us?"

We backpedaled. "We had no reason to believe anything other than what you told us until just now. No amount of screaming will wake up a baby that's not there."

Laura stepped in front of us, positioning her body between the carriage and us. "You want to see the baby?"

"Yes," we responded.

"You really want to see our baby and put an end to this absurdity?"

Again, we responded, "Yes."

With the care of a seamstress sewing on a button, she lifted the opaque canopy of the stroller.

We stared in silence.

Victor spoke first. "She's a 'believe baby.' You have to believe really hard and she will come to life. She only looks that way because you don't believe in her. If you believe in her she will open her eyes."

We stared at the emaciated remains of a child no larger than the forearm of a small woman.

"Don't worry. She looks like that when she is around nonbelievers," Laura said. "The agency said that she will come to life when you believe."

We tried to talk, but found ourselves speechless.

Finally, one of us spoke up, "So you're telling us that the baby was alive before we got here? And will be alive once we leave?"

They nodded in unison. "But if you believe, she will come alive for you, too. Just close your eyes and open your hearts."

We looked at each other. And then at Victor and Laura.

Fighting through the horror of it all, we dared ourselves to believe in the baby. We wanted to still believe in Victor and Laura.

In the silence of our wishful thinking, our heads bowed and our eyes tightly closed, we waited.

What we heard next would be the subject of debate in our direct group chats for months afterwards. We all agreed that we had heard the faint sound of a baby's gurgle and cooing, but we were divided as to whether the sounds came from the carriage just beyond our reach or the parents standing on either side of it.

TALONS

Her story went like this: When she was three years old, she was playing with her brother in the backyard, when an enormous hawk swooped down, latched on to her, and lifted her from the ground. The only thing that stopped her from being carried away was her brother grabbing hold of her legs and snatching her from the bird's grasp. The only evidence the incident had even occurred were the parallel, permanent scars left on her shoulders.

We had been dating for a month before she told me that story. I smiled and tried to play it off, but the whole thing disturbed me. For some reason I just couldn't shake the notion that my girlfriend was almost prey, that she could have been pecked to death by birds, her flesh stripped slowly from her small body.

The idea haunted me, even as we made love that first time. I could feel the slight raise of her skin when I scooped my hands around her shoulders and pulled her closer. Once I felt her scars, I was unable to remove my hands.

Each time we were intimate I'd rest my hands on those scars, sometimes imagining wings were beginning to sprout from them.

One night I awakened to find her straddling me, the darkness masking my ability to see clearly. I reached for her shoulders, but she eased my hands away. She made love to me, her hands gripping my arms like talons, pinning me in place. When she climaxed, I swore I could see wings unfurling from her shoulders against the night.

Not long after that, I realized I was not cut out for a relationship with her. Much of our relationship had been spent in the dark, and while I was unsure if what I thought I had seen was true, I could never overcome my fear she would one day clamp onto me and carry me off, somewhere deep into the night, where I would be devoured by a family of hawks, not unlike those who awaited her many years ago, my skin pecked from my body strip by strip.

THE GIRL WITH SILVER HAIR

Ayodele Hall's battered, old hatchback came to a squealing stop on the gravel in front of Sunnyvale Hospice Care. There wasn't much of a parking lot outside the small building, as it only housed ten beds, several of which were hardly ever used. She glanced in the mirror of her cracked sun visor, checking her hair to make sure it was presentable. This wig was a short crop, designed to place one in the mind of a young Halle Berry, although Ayodele wrestled with whether she had the confidence to pull it off.

She grabbed the literary journal from the passenger seat of her car and locked the door. Ms. Norma had asked Ayodele to bring one of her published stories to read the next time she visited. There had only been two of them in the five years that Ayodele had been writing, and she had yet to write a single page of her novel. She found herself, at times, embarrassed about her writing, feeling it wasn't good enough to be taken seriously. She had only acquiesced to Ms. Norma's request because the woman was one of the few people she actually talked to, not to mention she was terminally ill.

Ayodele had first met Ms. Norma during her candy-striping

days at the town's only hospital. That had been two years ago, when Ayodele started reading to swing-bed patients as a way of fighting loneliness. Ms. Norma had been one of the patients whose family members never came to visit, an elderly woman who could appreciate what it meant just to have someone sitting nearby. In the time since Ayodele had moved on from candy striping, she had continued visiting Ms. Norma, even after the old woman transferred to this grim-looking hospice.

There was absolutely nothing sunny about Sunnyvale, so Ayodele sometimes brought things to read to Ms. Norma on her visits. Once Ayodele let it slip she was a writer, the old woman demanded Ayodele bring in one of her own stories to read.

The literary journal felt like a stone tablet in Ayodele's hands. She didn't know why she was nervous about sharing something that had already been published. Maybe it was because Ms. Norman wasn't just some anonymous reader.

When Ayodele entered the room, she found Ms. Norma lying so vibrantly in her bed, the old woman's silver hair thick and cascading onto her shoulders. She was a picture of health, and Ayodele doubted she could be in the final days of any illness.

"You made it!" Ms. Norma said, her voice as full as the color in her walnut skin.

Ayodele nodded, lifting the journal weakly above her head, as if to say, *Well, here it is.*

"Girl, what are we gonna do with you? You're a rose. Don't shrink from the sun."

"Yes, ma'am."

"Hold your head up. You're too beautiful to be walking around with your shoulders scrunched up and your head down."

Ayodele nodded. She knew Ms. Norma's words were supposed to lift her spirits, but they actually made her feel worse. She was so homely and pathetic that an elderly woman had to give her advice on how to carry herself.

"I'm glad you brought your story, but I hope you don't mind if we just talk for a bit."

"Yes, ma'am."

"Have a seat," Ms. Norma said, pointing to the old wooden chair seated near her bed. "And pull up close. My energy comes and goes so fast these days."

Ayodele did as she was told.

"Aah," Ms. Norma said, smiling. "Look at you. I see so much of myself in you."

"How so?"

"When I was your age, I was still trying to figure it all out. My plan was to see the world—and I did, the good and the bad."

Ayodele smiled at the thought of traveling somewhere beyond the boring confines of her own town. "It must have been quite an adventure."

"I guess you could say that." Ms. Norma sighed. "At first I was pretty insecure. I guess I felt like I needed the approval of someone to know I was a beautiful and smart woman in the world. As time went on, it didn't matter so much to me anymore."

Ayodele nodded.

"I guess what I'm saying is you gotta be comfortable in your own skin before you can be comfortable in the world."

Ms. Norma rarely had this much to say to her, and rarely had it all been so applicable to Ayodele's life.

"Come close," Ms. Norma said.

Ayodele leaned in.

"Can I ask you a question?"

"Yes, ma'am."

"Why are you wearing a wig?"

The question took Ayodele aback for a moment, and she found herself staring at the old lady unable to formulate a response.

Reading her reaction, Ms. Norma continued, "I don't mean it in a bad way. I was just curious."

Aydoele pondered whether to open up to her or not. She trusted the old woman, and denying her felt like an unnecessary thing to do to someone not long for this world anyway.

"I have alopecia. When I was growing up, my grandmother had me getting perms or using a hot comb every other week, and, well," she paused, taking a deep breath, "it just took a toll."

Ms. Norma nodded, her look so tender and empathetic that Ayodele could not hold back her tears.

"Now, now," the old woman said. "It's okay."

"No, ma'am. It's not okay. It's hard. *Really hard.*" Now the tears were streaming down Ayodele's cheeks. She closed her eyes, and seconds later she could feel the soft hand of the old woman brushing her wet face.

"Don't cry," Ms. Norma said. "Hold your head up."

Ayodele wiped her face and looked into the eyes of the old woman, no longer able to hide her vulnerability.

"Can I see your head?" Ms. Norma asked, quietly.

"You want me to take off my wig?"

"Just for a moment. It's just the two of us here."

Ayodele nodded and slowly removed the wig from her head and yielded to the gentle touch of the old woman's soft, warm fingers touching her scalp. She thought she would flinch beneath the touch—after all, no one had touched her head in years—but she didn't.

Ms. Norma's hands moved over the bald and thinned spots, as well as the places where the hair remained thick and curly, and it felt good to be seen and touched by someone who did not judge her or think her ugly.

When the old woman finally removed her hand from Ayodele's scalp, Ayodele immediately craved the touch again. It was only after she had read her story to the old woman and hugged her with everything she had to offer that she placed the wig back on her head and walked back to her car, tears in her eyes, but her head held high.

As AYODELE lay in bed that night trying to sleep, her scalp itched beneath her night scarf. At first she tried to pat it gently, but eventually she used the tips of her fingers in an effort to satiate the discomfort. She briefly considered getting up and removing the scarf, maybe washing her hair in the shower, but she was far too tired to move. The day had drained her, both physically and emotionally. After a while, the itching subsided and she fell into a deep sleep.

She awoke the next morning and bypassed her usual coffee en route to her laptop. The morning writing was a ritual she had been trying out for several weeks, but this was the first morning she actually felt compelled to write something. In fact, she was overflowing with ideas. She typed for hours, and finally forced herself to stop so she could shower and prepare for her afternoon shift at the call center. It was only when she removed her scarf before entering the shower that she caught sight of her hair.

Contrasting sharply against her dark skin was hair so silver it seemed to actually move with the light's reflection. Its length touched her shoulder, and all of the spots where hair could no longer grow were now filled with thick, full, healthy silver hair. In that moment, she knew Ms. Norma had had something to do with this.

She stood there, staring at it, unable to believe her eyes. She quickly ran her fingers through the thick strands, from the roots all the way out to the ends. The mass of it was incredible. She looked like Storm (and even felt like her), and while the color made her age indeterminate, she refused to do anything to alter the gift she was given. To dye this beautiful mane would be sacrilege.

How had Ms. Norma done this? It made no sense, but in that moment, she was unable to contain the ecstatic feeling that she now had hair more perfect than any wig she had ever owned.

While dressing, she phoned Sunnyvale in hopes of being able to speak to Ms. Norma before she left for work. She hoped the old woman could explain everything to her, but when the receptionist answered the phone and immediately handed it off to one of the nurse practitioners, Ayodele felt an involuntary tightness take hold of her stomach.

"Hello?" Ayodele said. "I was wondering if I might be able to speak to Ms. Norma."

There was a pause, and in that silence she knew that Ms. Norma had passed. The nurse's words swept over her like a distant breeze, and she could not tell at what point she hung up the phone, sat down on the sofa, and cried as if she had lost a member of her own family.

She cried for the loss of her friend. She cried because she had, in many ways, taken the old woman for granted. She cried because the woman had seemed to give her something she had neither the mindset nor the wisdom to comprehend. But most of all, she cried because tears were all that were left when apologies could not find their mark.

Her crying only ceased when she was overcome with more ideas for stories. She felt guilty moving from one thing to the next, but had no logical reason why she shouldn't write at that moment. She sat down in front of her laptop and proceeded to write these new ideas.

It was only after she finished writing that she realized her new creative rush seemed to coincide with her new hair.

OVER THE NEXT TWO WEEKS, the feeling of loneliness that had often followed her home from her job had nearly ceased altogether. No sooner than she would enter her small apartment would she find herself sitting at her laptop, writing feverishly.

The work had begun to accumulate so quickly she had to create time to edit it and then look for places to submit it. A few years earlier she had joined a local writing group, her first real effort at workshopping her fiction. She soon discovered, however, the group divided up easily into four different personalities: (1) those who'd had a few pieces published and felt like they were the ultimate arbiters of all that was holy and publishable, (2) those who had literally just started writing and hadn't gotten past their first stories, (3) those who called themselves writers when all they really did was read and critique others for not being more like their favorite writers, and (4) those who just needed to get out of the house and into the hair of someone who wasn't his or her spouse. None of those factions appealed to Ayodele, and it didn't help that she was the only African American in the group. Most of what concerned them didn't concern her as much. In fact, the handful of pieces she had submitted to the workshop had been widely critiqued for not being "ethnic" enough. She had even been questioned as to why there were often no white people in her stories. One person went so far as to say, "The real world has white people in it, so you can't just write a story where there aren't any white people. That's not believable." It was shortly after that remark that Ayodele realized she didn't have the patience for trying to educate people who seemed to think the entirety of the African-American experience had to be framed against whiteness.

Things were a bit slow going after that. Eventually she learned to write, reflect over, and edit her own short stories. Her shelves housed a variety of grammar books, alongside books by authors whose mere existences raised her morale in ways that writing groups had not managed to do, writers like Octavia Butler, Nalo

Hopkinson, Tananarive Due, Zora Neale Hurston, Toni Morrison, Toni Cade Bambara, Nnedi Okorafor, and N.K. Jemisin. It wasn't enough for African Americans, in general, to exist in a speculative space; African-American women, in particular, needed to be a part of that space. It was the notion that she could see herself in the works of these women that she insulated herself from the confusion, rejection, patriarchy, and downright racism of many local white writers she had encountered.

The silver hair had changed a few things, though. What had once been a tediously slow creative process was now accelerated, like the hair was some sort of amphetamine—but she liked it, mainly because it gave her little time to grieve the loss of her friend and to get mired in feelings of loneliness.

In an attempt to slow down her racing mind, she took to writing longhand. After depleting what she had at home, she drove downtown to the local bookstore, a place that seemed like it sold more coffee than books. Usually she loved bookstores—saw them as a sanctuary of sorts from the rest of the world—but she disliked the notion that books could be props for people to sit around and drink expensive cups of coffee. Still, this was one of the few places that sold the kind of hardback notebooks that she preferred.

There was a smattering of people across the store, most of them seated in the cafe area drinking coffee and reading books they had no plans to actually buy. Ayodele quickly found her notebooks and grabbed five of them, along with a few pens that could easily clip onto the books. As she held them gingerly in the crook of her arm, she noticed a section of writing magazines on the periodicals rack. She grabbed several of them and quickly made her purchase, before heading back home.

During the entire drive, her mind raced with ideas. All of the ideas seemed to revolve around this one small Southern town. It was as if she knew everyone who lived there. She even knew the name: Sugarville. There was a map of the place in her head, and she wondered briefly if Faulkner's commitment to setting his works in Yoknapatawpha County was the result of what she was now experiencing.

She uncapped one of the pens and unwrapped the plastic from one of the journals, opening it to the first page. Ink danced onto the page and Ayodele smiled.

❦

To give herself a break, Ayodele decided to take a bubble bath. She couldn't comfortably write in the tub, with either the laptop or a notebook, and that was fine by her. It also gave her some time and space to review the writing magazines she had purchased. Many of them were known for having publishing opportunities listed in the backs. Maybe she would find somewhere she could submit her work. She doubted she had enough for a full collection of short stories, but she could still send out individual pieces in hopes of finding a home for one or two.

When Ayodele was into the third magazine, she noticed a fellowship opportunity with a rolling deadline. It seemed so perfect that she considered if the universe had created this opportunity specifically for her. Even better, there was no application fee. Two weeks in a scenic town, all expenses paid, plus a stipend, and a place to stay? Ayodele had vacation time she had not yet taken, so if she were fortunate enough to win this fellowship, she would have no problem making it happen. She poured over every detail in the advertisement: the Daylight Fellowship was an opportunity to visit the community of Daylight, Mississippi, where you would be housed in a small townhouse downtown to do your writing, have access to all of the local businesses and restaurants, and have plenty of time to write. All you had to do, outside of coming and writing, was present an official reading at

the local public library. One thing that stood out even more than
the rest was that the instructions stated explicitly that women of
color were welcome to apply.

Once she got out of the tub and dried off, she combed
through her latest writings to see if she had the twenty-page
sample that was requested to accompany the application. Once
she settled on a few pieces, she edited them until she grew so
tired she could no longer stay awake.

On her way to work the next day, she dropped her application in the mail, crossed her fingers, and hoped that her good
fortune would continue.

THE SPEED of the acceptance letter surprised her. She couldn't
remember exactly when she had mailed it, and because of her
feverish writing, she had lost track of time. Still, something in her
seemed to acknowledge that things had happened rather quickly.

The letter came in a small envelope, the opposite of what she
had expected. It was congratulatory and offered a phone number
to speak with someone at the Daylight Foundation about setting
up her flight arrangements. The check was to be awarded once
she arrived. She would also receive the key to her townhouse once
she was picked up from the airport by a member of the Daylight
Foundation. Because she had never won a fellowship of any kind
before, she didn't know what the proper protocol was for this
type of thing, but even if she did know, she figured it would
differ from place to place. What she did know, however, was that
she had won her first writing fellowship and would be able to
leave her drab Virginia apartment for a nice writing nook in
Mississippi.

As she'd expected, she had no problem getting her vacation
days approved, even on such short notice, so she made her travel

arrangements, packed her things into a large suitcase, and prepared for what she hoped would surely be one of the major adventures of her life.

THE JUNE BREEZE seemed to beckon Ayodele as she stepped off the plane in Daily, Mississippi, roughly half an hour from Daylight. The airport in Daily was so small that only one plane could arrive in a two-hour window. The plane had been so small she feared the pilot would come over the intercom and tell everyone on the left side of the plane to stick their arms out the windows and flap them to keep the plane in the air. A relief settled over her when she saw a small, round woman with glasses and a teeny-weeny afro jumping up and down with a poster that read "Ayodele Hall." Ayodele immediately began walking toward her.

"Hi, Ms. Hall. I'm Bernetta Jamison, and I work with the Daylight Foundation. I just wanted to welcome you to Mississippi!"

Ayodele smiled and shook the woman's hand. "I'm glad to be here."

"I will be taking you to Daylight to get you checked into your place. Let's grab your luggage and head on to Daylight."

Bernetta spoke and walked so quickly, Ayodele had trouble keeping up with both. No sooner than her bag tumbled down onto the baggage claim conveyor did Bernetta grab it. Ayodele had to ask herself if she had even identified the bag to the woman. She figured she had. How she would be able to keep up with Bernetta's energy was beyond her.

The two of them hopped into Bernetta's compact hatchback and pulled out of the airport parking lot.

"That silver hair," Bernetta started, "it's a good look on you."

"Thanks."

"We'll be in Daylight in about thirty minutes, so just sit back and rest yourself. Enjoy the scenery."

Ayodele nodded, but once she had seen what felt like the one millionth tree lining the highway in the first ten minutes of the drive, she closed her eyes and yielded to the nap she had been unable to embrace on her flight.

She woke up as Bernetta pulled into downtown Daylight, and what she saw nearly made her scream when she looked through the car window.

❧

ALMOST TO THE LETTER, the town of Daylight looked like what she had imagined Sugarville to be when she was writing. It was as if her imagination had come to life. Not having seen a single picture of Daylight, although she could have done a search online before coming, she immediately knew where everything was. Seeing the town in person made her wonder if any of the stories she had written were about any real citizens. She shook her head, refusing to believe this could be anything other than a coincidence.

Once they pulled up to her townhouse, just off the town square, Bernetta reached into her purse and pulled out an envelope and handed it to Ayodele.

"We will be hosting a reception for you tonight over at the public library, which is a short walk from here. Call me if you need anything in the meantime. You have my number."

"Thank you."

Ayodele opened the envelope and saw a house key sitting atop at least three hundred dollars in twenty-dollar bills.

"That's your food per diem for the time you're here. Let me

know if you need anything or want to go anywhere farther than walking distance."

"Sure thing," Ayodele responded, looking down at the money again. "I'll see you this evening."

"All right," Bernetta said, waving wildly from behind the steering wheel.

Ayodele took her things up to the door and unlocked it. She smiled as she looked inside and saw that it was perfect for writing. A large bookshelf lined the wall and an antique mahogany roll-top desk sat across from it. It looked like the kind of place one could write the Great American Novel, and she could barely contain her joy.

She quickly put her things away and locked up the townhouse. With a few hours to spare, she figured she would explore this strange new place that would be her home for the next two weeks. But more than that, she was curious as to how much of this place matched with her imagination.

❦

SOME PLACES LOOKED EXACTLY like Sugarville, but other places looked entirely different. She couldn't make heads or tails of it, so she decided to just focus on getting to know her new surroundings with an open mind. Since both the opening reception and her presentation the following week were taking place at the Daylight Public Library, Ayodele decided it was probably best to locate it first and then orient herself to the rest of the town from there.

The library was on the other side of the town square. It looked like a miniature brick castle and was easily the most interesting building in the area. It looked both old and new at the same time, as if part of the structure had existed for decades and the other part was a recent addition. The brick colors and patterns were so fluid, though, it was difficult to tell which came first.

Across from the library sat the Daylight Police Station, which housed three empty police cars that looked like they had been unoccupied for quite some time. The street was relatively quiet with the occasional car that seemed to roll down the street in no particular hurry. The town was quite beautiful, and she immediately saw how such an environment could further spark her creativity—as if her hair hadn't done enough already.

She walked up the handful of steps to the library's grand entrance. The inside was far less impressive. At a glance Ayodele could tell that there weren't a lot of books on the shelves. The place was also very drab and dimly lit, as if everything amazing about the building had been put into its exterior, as opposed to the things that took place under its roof. There were only three people sitting at the tables in the main area, and they were seated at computers that were so old looking they had long rear casings on the monitors that looked like egg shell-colored E.T. heads. Ayodele wondered, with no humor, if the machines still ran DOS, as opposed to any operating system developed in the twenty-first century. She had been standing in the center of the library's main space for less than a minute and could not imagine the building hosting any kind of reception. Ayodele had seen restrooms at truck stops that had more potential.

She walked through the stacks slowly, glancing from shelf to barren shelf. She noticed a woman standing by a cart at the end of a row, a pencil tucked behind her ear. The woman was looking at her curiously, and she imagined they mirrored the same expression.

"Excuse me, ma'am. I'm in town visiting, and I was wondering if you had a reference room, something with local resources about the community. See, I'm doing some research and just wanted to learn more about this place."

The woman looked at her for a moment, then glanced around as if she were being watched. "We don't have a reference room," she finally responded.

Ayodele looked through the gap in the shelves and noticed a room that clearly seemed like it was designated as a reference room. "What about that one over there?"

The woman once again glanced around before speaking. "You have to have authorization to go in there."

Ayodele's brows furrowed. "Well, how do I get authorization?"

The woman nervously tapped her fingers against the book cart. "Hey, I just want to finish putting these books up. I have to go."

Before Ayodele could respond, the woman grabbed her cart and almost ran away with it across the room.

Part of Ayodele wanted to seek out a manager or to run over to the woman and check her on her behavior, but she was not the confrontational type, she knew, and she figured she could just try again when she came to the reception later. Then maybe she would report the woman to her superiors.

Ayodele decided to leave the library and head back to her townhouse. Daylight was a little stranger than she had imagined, and she wasn't entirely sure if she liked that or not. Still, she had been given a fellowship for her art, so maybe things would improve.

She certainly hoped so.

AYODELE HAD NOT CONSIDERED if her townhouse had a back-door until she heard a rhythmic rapping against the wood. At first she took the sound for that of a woodpecker in the distance or some kid knocking about in the alley behind the townhouses on that street, but then she got curious. She figured it must have been a nosy neighbor trying to see who the new person was, so she braced herself to open the door.

Standing directly in front of the backdoor was a small, slender old woman with a gray Caesar haircut, wearing a pair of green sweatpants and a t-shirt that read "Don't Hate Me Because I'm Flyy."

"Ayodele, I'm Georgia. Can I come in?"

She stared at the old woman, wondering how the woman knew her name.

"I need to come in now. Norma Jean sent me," the woman said.

Ayodele backed away from the door, allowing the old woman into the kitchen space that occupied the back of the house.

"Can I help you?"

"I know you don't know me from a hole in the wall, but I need you to be quiet for a minute and listen to everything I'm about to tell you because we don't have much time."

GEORGIA SAT down across from Ayodele at the small kitchen table, crossing her legs before she spoke. "Norma Jean has been telling me about you. She told me that she had given you her power and that she would be passing on. But she feared for your safety. That's why I'm here."

"I'm lost. What are you talking about?" Ayodele said.

Georgia leaned in closer. "The woman with silver hair is always the sacrifice, and you've been lured here as a sacrifice.

"Roughly forty-five years ago Norma Jean was lured to this town to be a sacrifice, and she would have been, except I helped her to escape. I'm here to help you escape, too."

Stunned and confused, Ayodele looked at Georgia. This

woman must be crazy, she thought, looking at her smartphone and suddenly realizing she didn't have any service or access to Wi-Fi. She scanned the room to see if there was a landline, but she couldn't find one. She figured if things got too crazy with the old woman, she would flip over the table and maybe throw something at her before she ran away.

"I know this is a bit much to swallow, but it's the truth. You've had visions of this place, haven't you?"

Ayodele nodded slowly.

"That's what the hair does. It wants to bring you here."

"But I won a fellowship through a literary journal," Ayodele said.

"That's how they lure you in. The hair deepens your well of creativity, while connecting you to Sugarville. They run that ad year-round in all of these literary and art journals in hopes of getting someone who submits some kind of sample that speaks about the town."

The word "Sugarville" hung in the air.

"This is Sugarville. It's not Daylight?"

"Daylight is the name they changed the town to after I helped Norma Jean escape. The town is broke from years of running the ads and trying to keep up appearances. The only way back to prosperity is through sacrificing the woman with silver hair."

Ayodele shook her head. Georgia was saying just enough for her to not entirely dismiss her, but still none of it made any sense.

"How exactly am I supposed to be a sacrifice? This is 2019! Surely people don't do that kind of thing. Do they want the hair? If they do, they can have it."

"The prosperity of Sugarville has always been tied to sacrifices to a monster we call Mwovu. The town was founded by a small group of newly freed slaves who negotiated to buy their former master's plantation shortly before he died with no heirs. Legend has it that they bought the land for a dollar—and that they borrowed that dollar from their master. Anyway, a lot of the white folks didn't take too kindly to black folks owning all that land, so they set about trying to scare folks into leaving. It was then that a strange man walked through the town one day and said that he had a way to solve their problem and protect their land for generations."

Ayodele shook her head. "This sounds like some really bad story that someone made up."

"It's all true. I swear," said Georgia. "The guy brought a seed and planted it in the earth, and from that seed Mwovu grew. He comes every generation for his sacrifice, and although you can't probably tell from the look of it, the town is way overdue. Most of this place is falling apart completely. People were starting to get pretty desperate before you came."

"And the hair?" Ayodele asked.

"Mwovu doesn't want just the hair. It wants the head of the sacrifice."

The scream leaped from Ayodele's lips so fast that should could not stop herself. "These people brought me here to kill me?"

Georgia nodded. "That's why I'm gonna help you get out of here before the ritual tonight."

Ayodele's blood felt cold in her veins, her stomach cramping from fear and her legs giant blocks of concrete. She wanted to run away from it all, but she didn't know where to start. She had flown out here to the middle of nowhere—and then been driven a good thirty miles farther into God knows where. Her smart phone was useless at this point. She had no transportation besides her feet. Even worse, it seemed like the entire town was in on it.

"If what you're saying is true, then why are you trying to help me and not deliver me to Mwovu?"

Georgia lowered her head. "The truth? I just feel like we can't keep feeding evil, giving it what it wants, you know? Maybe someone should just burn this place to the ground so we can start over, but no one wants to do that."

Ayodele steadied her voice. "So does anyone know you helped Ms. Norma escape?"

"If they did, I wouldn't be here. They would've gotten rid of me a long time ago. You only have to see one person sacrificed to know that this whole thing is wrong. I just can't let it happen again, even if that means the end for this place. I can't say that I haven't prayed that the earth would just open up and swallow Sugarville whole."

Ayodele's legs bounced up and down nervously. She had been trying to resist everything this woman was saying, to reject all of its craziness, but she realized that it didn't matter if it were true or not. This was a free country, and she didn't have to stay anywhere she didn't want to. She just needed for this woman to help her get back to Daily. She could take it from there.

"So how do we get out of here?" she asked.

Georgia nodded knowingly. "It won't be easy."

❦

AYODELE HOPED that no one saw her creep into the backseat of Georgia's old station wagon. She lay on the floor, her body bent at an odd angle, her face pressed against old lost French fries and other car grit. As the car moved slowly down the road, she kept glancing at her phone, the battery already below fifty percent, hoping she would be able to pick up some kind of signal.

"If the hair is magic, how does it fit into any of this?" she asked, talking beneath the seat.

"I don't know where the silver hair came from. I don't know if anyone does. We only know that somehow it's connected to Mwovu and that this land is the conduit.

"I kept in contact with Norma Jean for years after she left, and she said nothing ever came for her, wherever she was. I think there's something about this land that's sacred. Like the hair and the land are some kind of lock and key for Mwovu to grow. I don't know. I'm not sure anyone does. People just do what they are supposed to do because someone who died before they were even born told them to. Isn't that the way it is with most things?"

Ayodele didn't know what kind of answer that was to her question, but it further added to the notion that she needed to just keep her peace until she could get back to Daily.

For a while the car crept along in silence. Suddenly Georgia pumped the car's brakes and Ayodele rolled into the base of the front seats.

"What is it?" she asked, spitting away the detritus pressed into her lips.

"There's a roadblock up ahead…a few hundred yards away."

"What do we do?"

"Ease onto the backseat and reach for the blanket in the back, behind the seat. Pull it down on top of you and don't say a thing."

Ayodele did as she was instructed and pulled the heavy, funky blanket down on top of herself. The scent was so horrendous, she lifted the scoop of her shirt's neckline and lowered her nose beneath it, hoping to catch the smell of lotion on her own body.

"Hang in there," Georgia said, "and make sure that you're completely covered, no spaces."

She could hardly breathe from the heat and the musty smell of the blanket. She turned her face beneath the seat, leaving a small gap so she could get a sliver of the car's air conditioning and some clean air.

The car came to a complete stop again, and there was a knocking sound on the driver's window. Ayodele closed her mouth tightly for fear that her breathing might be audible.

"Georgia, where are you headed this evening? You know the ritual is in another hour. You need to be getting back home," a gravely voice said.

"I have to run out and pick up a few things for tonight," Georgia responded.

"Well, they're having trouble locating the girl. They said she went to the library and then she went back to the townhouse. Now no one can seem to find her. We've been told to check all cars headed east out of town, just in case someone gets the stupid idea of ruining the sacrifice tonight."

"That's just downright ridiculous," Georgia said.

Ayodele prayed like hell the person outside the car was buying what Georgia was saying, because she sure wasn't.

"Well," the gravely voice said, "don't take this the wrong way, but I'm going to have do a K9 sweep of your car. I'm sorry for the inconvenience."

"Don't worry about it," Georgia said. "I understand."

A second later the back door, inches from Ayodele, popped open and she could hear the sniffing sounds of an animal hovering over her.

"All right. Everything looks clear," the gravely voice said, but out of nowhere the dog started bark maniacally.

"You got something back here, Georgia?" the voice said, and then in one swift swoop, the blanket was yanked from her body, leaving her exposed to a German Shepherd leaping at her, teeth bared.

"We got her," Ayodele heard the muscular policewoman say into her walkie-talkie, as Georgia sobbed heavily in the front seat.

Ayodele could barely make out Georgia's words, but once she was loaded into the back of the police car, her mind put those utterances together: "I told you to cover yourself *completely!*"

As the police car drove slowly through the streets of downtown Daylight, the sun began to set. Ayodele could see hundreds of people lining the sidewalks, as if she were the main float in a parade. It was only when she saw everyone altogether that she realized the entire town was African American. Little kids waved, their brown faces smiling in anticipation of what would be their first sacrifice. The adults looked on somberly.

Ayodele lunged against the cage in the backseat, screaming. The handcuffs holding her wrists behind her back felt as if they were digging through her skin into her bones. "You can't do this! Someone help me!"

She didn't know if the people along the route could hear her behind the window, and if they could, would it have mattered? According to them, they were on the eve of prosperity—whatever that meant.

The police car parked in the lot across the street from the library, and the policewoman emerged from the front of the car, opened the back door, and yanked Ayodele from the car to loud applause from the onlookers.

"Get up off the ground. Have some dignity about yourself," the woman said lifting Ayodele to her feet from her fetal position on the ground.

Once they began the slow, excruciating trek across the street, Ayodele scanned the crowd for Georgia. She didn't know what had happened to her once the police took her, but she silently hoped Georgia would be in the crowd for the ritual. She desperately needed to have a familiar, helpful face nearby.

The dim light of the library was replaced with an almost daylight glow reflected from the hundreds of candles forming a large circle in the center of the main room. In the middle of the circle was a wooden chair that appeared to be bolted to the floor. Ropes rested on either side of the chair. Ayodele knew immediately that they would be used to bind her there.

Her heart racing, she scanned the crowd repeatedly, all while trying to keep from crying. She needed her vision to see, and every tear or drop of sweat would prevent her from doing this.

"Georgia!" she yelled out over the cacophony. "Georgia!"

The thought that the old woman had been either detained or had left Sugarville began to weigh heavily on her mind. Surely, she was among this raucous crowd.

The officer marched her over to the chair and pushed her down into the seat. Bernetta, her ride into town, emerged from the crowd holding a large leather-bound book. People moved swiftly to replace Ayodele's handcuffs with the ropes, shifting her hands to her lap. Within minutes she was even more bound than she had been in the back of the patrol car.

"Georgia," she moaned, as the idea that she was now alone in all of this dawned over her.

Then between the people jostling back and forth outside the circle for a better view, she caught a glimpse of Georgia bobbing up and down trying to get her attention.

A clock tolled from somewhere outside the building and a hush fell over the room. Bernetta then took her place a few feet to the side of Ayodele and opened the leather-bound book.

"In honor of he who is greater than we are, we humbly submit this silver-haired sacrifice to you." Bernetta then closed the book and turned to face Ayodele. "You will bring prosperity to this town. Your sacrifice will not be in vain."

It took everything in Ayodele to not scream again. She need to remain as calm as possible.

"Bernetta, may I have a final word?"

Bernetta looked to the elders who stood just outside the circle and they nodded in unison. "Okay, but be brief because Mwovu will be here soon."

The ground beneath the library began to vibrate with a low, audible buzz and Ayodele's feet trembled. She had only one plan, and she prayed it would work.

"Georgia," she called out. "Please. There is something I have to tell you before it comes."

Georgia stepped forward into the circle and stood directly in front of her.

"Thank you—for everything," Ayodele said.

Georgia nodded and smiled, and as the floor began to rumble, she quickly knelt in front of Ayodele and Ayodele placed her hands onto the old woman's scalp. The two of them had planned this as a last resort, and now Ayodele prayed that it would work.

Looking down at Georgia, she felt dread take hold of her. Then, almost all at once, the old woman's gray hair turned a brilliant silver and Ayodele's hair began to tighten into the short coils she had covered for many years of her life.

"Now!" yelled Ayodele, and Georgia sprinted into the crowd touching the heads of every woman she could reach in the crowd.

The potency of the touch was apparently much stronger in Sugarville because the room was suddenly aglow with the rippling heads of at least ten women. People began to scream as they, themselves, began reaching for other scalps within their own reach.

Suddenly, in all the chaos, the ground beneath the outer edge of the circle exploded and opened up. In the middle of the fallen debris stood a tiny boy, his hair as golden as the sun and his skin the color of snow. The room fell silent as they gazed at the being who had not set foot on the soil of Sugarville in more than a generation.

The little boy looked at Ayodele quizzically, confused at her appearance. Then something caught his eye and he noticed the rippling hair in the crowd. He inhaled deeply and his body increased in mass until his height rose above the heads of all present. He jaws widened to the length of his shoulders. Then he sprinted toward the crowd.

Cries filled the room as people broke into every direction. In the melee, Georgia ran to Ayodele and untied her ropes. The two of them eased out of the library through the side entrance.

When Ayodele stepped into the night air, she could still hear the gargling screams and the bone snapping of carnage in the distance.

⚝

As THEY TRAVELED through the blackness of the country road, neither woman spoke. Since they had pulled away from Sugarville there had been not a single light. It was as if the town had disappeared in the distance. When finally the night lights of Daily approached, Ayodele released a long sigh she didn't realize she had been holding.

"What will you do now?" Ayodele finally asked.

"Go back and see what remains of the town at some point. I'll figure out what to do then."

Ayodele nodded.

"Girl, that hair was really something else," Georgia said laughing. "How did I look? My hair hadn't been that long in ages. Probably better that I didn't have a chance to get used to it."

Ayodele smiled, but her heart was still racing. Everything had happened so quickly that she was just now digesting what had taken place in the last twelve hours.

"I'm guessing I won't be able to get a flight out of here anytime soon," she said.

"There's always Memphis," Georgia said. "They're a much bigger airport."

"You don't mind driving all the way to Memphis?"

"Where else do I have to be?"

Ayodele stared out of the windshield at the highway ahead of them.

"Thank you," she finally said.

"It's the least I could do for Norma Jean."

It was then that Ayodele understood the real reason why Georgia had saved Ms. Norma—and now her. It filled her heart with a warmth that allowed her to close her eyes and, for the first time, truly mourn her friend.

As the station wagon pushed forward, the night highway lay open before them, welcoming them into the safety of the unknown.

THE LOVE BALLOON

Nasir had bought the balloon at one of those party supply stores across the bridge in the next borough. It was four letters conjoined so they spelled out "LOVE," and the resulting balloon was enormous. The sales associate had to open both of the front doors, and the two of them jostled the balloon until, finally, it popped out on the other side.

The taxi Nasir took back into The City couldn't hold the balloon, so he held the thick cord through the window as the balloon floated above the car. He had the driver take him straight to Khadijah's apartment. It was only when he was standing on the sidewalk in front of her building that it suddenly hit him that the balloon would be far too big to fit in her place.

Nasir reached in his pocket and pulled out his phone. After two rings, Khadijah answered and he asked if she could come downstairs.

He stood alone on the sidewalk with his balloon. The only thing keeping her from seeing his surprise in advance was that her apartment was on the backside of the building, facing another street.

She had joked that he wasn't very spontaneous, so this was his chance to show her he could be just that. The balloon was too obvious to be considered a metaphor, but clearly that was the original idea. That the store even carried a balloon that size was in itself a bit surprising. The sales associate had said it was the store's attempt to capitalize on the LOVE sculptures being adopted by various cities throughout the country. Of course, the balloon was intended to be purchased still in the package and blown up later at the site of whatever event was taking place, but Nasir had convinced the associate to sell it to him fully blown up. His desire to confess his feelings for Khadijah had clouded his judgment a bit, causing him to forget he would look like a guy carrying a Macy's Thanksgiving Day balloon up the street.

When Khadijah got downstairs, she stared in amazement at the balloon's size.

"Wow!" was all she could manage, looking right past him and up the cord into the sky above his head.

"This is for you."

She didn't have to ask what it was or what it meant. She only stared at it.

"Here," he said, offering her the cord in his hand. "It's light. The helium, well, you know."

"Nas, I don't really know what I would do with something so *big*. But I thank you."

"That's what *she* said!" he responded, eager to avoid the panic of her rejection with a little levity.

She smiled, glanced at the dumb look on his face, and returned her eyes to the balloon.

"That's a lot of love."

"Yeah."

"*A lot* of love," she repeated.

"I just wanted to let you know how I felt about you. I'm a

good guy. I work hard. I'm faithful. I'm all the things you said you wanted in a man. Let me be that for you."

Khadijah returned her focus to his face. "You want to be that for me?"

"Yes. And more."

He extended the cord to her again. This time she reached out slowly and placed her hand above his, grasping the cord.

"I don't know where I'm going to put this balloon, though," she said, as he gently let go so she could take it.

In that moment it appeared she had grown right before his eyes, until he glanced down and noticed her feet had left the ground.

"Hold on," he said, reaching for her, but at that exact moment a gust of wind pulled her from his grasp, sweeping her up into the air. In seconds she was far above the trees.

Nasir chased after her from the ground, but the balloon kept pulling her higher and higher.

By the time he reached the end of the street, he could no longer see her. She had floated away.

Later, when he returned home and still had not heard from her, he pondered where she might be, secretly hoping that she had not let go.

THE SALVATORE GRANT

The walk to Salvatore's was a little over six miles across town, and Eddie Brown had decided to wear his only suit and a pair of pleather cap-toed Oxfords to the interview. His mother had told him that people didn't get a second chance to make a first impression, and he badly needed what Salvatore's had to offer.

Doing his best to ignore the steadily increasing May heat, he tried to imagine how the interview would go. He had never met anyone who had gone through the process, and had only become aware of the opportunity from a cryptic flyer that had been posted in the lobby of the public library. The flyer had seemed almost tailor-made for him: *Are you looking for money for college? Trying to get out of debt? Looking to buy a home? Call us!* He was in the former category, having just received an admissions letter from Yale, with no possible way of covering the massive difference that was left after the small scholarship he had received. His mother told him that he should be proud of himself that he had gotten into an Ivy League school and that would possibly help him to secure more money from one of the local state schools. But once he had seen the sharp letterhead of Yale University, he'd been unable to stop thinking about the school. And then he came across the flyer. Maybe it was all fate that he would report to New Haven, Connecticut, in the fall.

The woman Eddie had spoken to on the phone, after hearing his desperate story, had asked him to share information about his health. Did he have high blood pressure? Did he have diabetes? Were there any major medical issues in his family? The list seemed endless, and when he finally asked why the information was important, she responded that it was required information for all donations. She then went on to explain the process, sparing him no details of how the Salvatore Grant worked. He nearly dropped the phone several times during her spiel and had spent the rest of the week thinking about what she had said.

Finally, three days later, he had called the woman back, unable to tolerate his mother's attempts to sway his life in a different direction. He had earned a spot in the incoming class at Yale, and according to what the woman had told him, he would be well compensated. He had to take the chance.

Now, as he walked up the sidewalk to the skyscraper that housed Salvatore's, he tried to steel his nerves. Few accomplishments came without sacrifices, he told himself, as he entered the lobby.

"I'm Eddie Brown," he said to the receptionist. "I have a noon appointment."

The receptionist checked his name against her computer and pointed him to a row of chairs in the waiting area.

As he sat in one of the chic black leather chairs lining the room, he rocked his feet back and forth in his shoes, feeling the muscles in his legs tense. The polyester of his suit rubbed against his damp skin, and he took deep breaths to calm himself down. He was told by the woman on the phone that the interview was a formality. Still, Eddie didn't want to take any chances. He *had* to get this grant.

Five minutes later, as the large and small hands of the ornate analog clock lined up on twelve, a tall thin man in a bespoke suit emerged from the main door just off the reception area. He walked over to Eddie.

"Mr. Brown," he said, extending his hand to Eddie, "my name is Ignatius Esposito."

Eddie shook it, hoping his hands weren't as clammy as he feared they were.

"Follow me," Ignatius said.

The two of them walked through the door, down a long hall, to a bank of elevators. Once the doors closed, Ignatius placed his hands against a sensor and stepped back. The elevator began to rise until it reached the penthouse floor. Eddie took a deep breath as he stepped off the elevator behind his host.

"Please. Have a seat," Ignatius said, pointing to a seat at the end of a long table. On either side were a small group of people, hunched over notebooks and laptops. Ignatius took the empty seat closest to Eddie.

"Mr. Brown, I have brought members of the legal, medical, and culinary teams to address any questions you may have before we complete the contract and begin the procedure." Ignatius lifted several documents and perused them. "So you are going with the thigh option, I see."

"Yes," Eddie responded, his voice barely audible.

"And it's just one leg," Ignatius continued.

"Yes."

"Very smart. So do you have any questions for us?"

"How much of my thigh are you taking?" Eddie asked.

A woman on the right side of the table leaned forward to respond. Eddie figured she was one of the medical team. "We will remove a one-inch by one-inch block of flesh, then close you up. The physical therapy is included in the agreement."

Eddie took a long, deep breath. "Will I still be able to walk?"

"Although you will have to make adjustments, with some effort and physical therapy you will retain your ability to walk," she said.

"Any other questions?" Ignatius asked.

"Yes," Eddie responded. "Can you walk me through what happens after the muscle tissue is removed from my thigh?"

"Sure," Ignatius said. "Chef Dino, could you explain the process for Mr. Brown, please."

"Well," Dino responded, leaning forward, "as you know, Salvatore's is an incredibly high-end restaurant. We cater to the most elite clientele in the world. As such, we provide the rarest of Italian foods. Among our specialties is the Salvatore's Chef Special Pizza, which consists of only the finest and rarest of ingredients: Pule cheese, white truffles, Lambda olive oil, a sauce made from Mexican Honey tomatoes, Charapita chilis, black squid ink dough, and of course the meat—courtesy of you. It is the fact that we cater to this high-end clientele that allows us to offer you a grant of this magnitude. Because your patron is in fact a Yale alum, part of your compensation will be taken care of directly by him. Salvatore's will compensate you $150,000 in cash, half upon the signing of the contract, the remainder after the procedure has been completed."

"So he's going to eat the muscle from my thigh?" Eddie's question was largely rhetorical, as everyone at the table knew the answer to that question, including Eddie. It was the thing that had given him pause before he arrived, but he had managed to push this final component into the back of his mind. After all, once the doctors removed the muscle from his leg, it would be waste. Why should he care what would be done with it at that point? Still, it was a difficult thought to *digest*, if he allowed himself to really go there.

"That is correct," Ignatius said. "This is a voluntary agreement on your part, and you are in no way under any obligation or coercion to comply. If, however, you choose to decline this offer, you are still bound by the signed non-disclosure agreement you emailed to us earlier this week."

Eddie flexed his legs beneath the table. He tried to imagine what it would be like to have a one-inch block of muscle removed from one of them. It wouldn't stop him from reading or writing or doing all that would be required of him to be successful at Yale. He would also have a connection to an alum, and that alone had a value that exceeded money.

He thought about what his mother might say if she knew he was in this room discussing giving up flesh from his thigh so that another man, a much wealthier and more powerful man, could ingest it on a pizza. He knew she would be horrified by the mere thought of it, but Eddie knew something at age eighteen that his mother probably didn't: the world was full of darkness, of those who had and those who didn't, and if it meant that he had to make this small sacrifice to gain acceptance into this world, that's what he would do.

"So do we have a deal?" Ignatius asked.

Eddie looked around the table at the faces awaiting his response, while running his sweating hands down the pleats of his slacks so that they rested on his thighs. He squeezed his legs, almost pinching them, then nodded. "Yes. We have a deal."

At that point the individuals whom Eddie assumed were a part of the legal team slid a manilla folder down the table to Ignatius and he perused it before pushing it over to Eddie and handing him a Montblanc to sign his signature.

Eddie took the pen in his hands, took a deep breath, and placed the nib of the fountain pen against the page, the crimson ink releasing as if the pen itself were a scalpel neatly separating the flesh of some poor, desperate soul—someone not unlike himself.

HAINT

"The death of a beautiful woman is questionably the most poetical
topic in the world."
~ Edgar Allan Poe

M y girlfriend is a ghost. Okay, I'm exaggerating a bit.
She's not my girlfriend—but she *is* a ghost.
Maybe I'm getting a little ahead of myself,
though. It's not everyday that someone enters into a relationship
with a ghost. This situation didn't come about like some Sam
Wheat-sliding-a-penny-up-a-door-and-making-Molly-cry-croc-
odile-tears-type of thing. Nor did it start at some singles' bar
where the living and dead take turns buying each other drinks in
hopes of that end-of-the-evening ethereal lay. No, my situation
started a bit more mundanely. Maybe you'd think me a little less
crazy if you heard the whole story. At least I hope so.

Shortly after I graduated from college, I decided to move to
Port Hilton, a small town off the eastern coast of Virginia. Up till
that point, I had only seen pictures of the city online and in the

occasional travel magazine. Still, I thought it a wonderfully picturesque place to begin my career as a novelist, especially since the city was quaint and surrounded by water on three sides.

My older brother, Satchel, thought me a fool for using the money from my trust fund in what he deemed a reckless fashion. "I'm just telling you what Mom and Dad would say if they were here. You should hold off on touching that money until you have a clearer idea of what you want to do in life." And for dramatic effect, he added, "If you blow through the money they left you, don't come looking to borrow from me."

Satchel and I couldn't be more dissimilar. He had already dipped, generously I might add, into his own trust fund to start a real estate business, the type of endeavor my parents would've surely approved of. To his credit, though, he had turned that million dollars into several million. These days, however, he is leveraged to the hilt, still trying to see his way clear of the punctured housing bubble.

What he refused to say in his counseling of me was that it was easy to lose money. But he needn't have said that. We were both hyperaware of my father's mantra: Don't be one of those fools who spends the first dollar of that million and is never a millionaire again.

I'm not sure my father would have approved of my chosen vocation, but I know my mother would have. She loved literature, and if I were to allow myself to believe that she and my father were still alive after their yacht disappeared off the coast of Madagascar six years ago, I would like to think she would encourage my decision.

My brother and I held a funeral for them a year after they disappeared, but that was strictly to help in our grieving process. The state requires seven years before my parents can officially be declared deceased, unless their bodies or the yacht turn up somewhere. So in a year, Satchel and I will be able to put all of this to rest—at least on paper. Incidentally, though, there might be another potential financial windfall, accompanied by all the things that go with probating their estates. Honestly, though, I'm not looking forward to any of that. Knowing my parents like I do (*did?*), they probably planned to leave their estates to various charities scattered around the world—something of which I'm completely cool with. The trust fund is more than sufficient.

There's a part of me that still thinks they might be alive out there somewhere. Maybe they found an island and decided to go off the grid. My father had set up the trust for us years ago, so maybe he knew ahead of time that he and Mom would disappear for a while.

But six years?

That's far too long to go without even sending a postcard. Even a message in a bottle would have arrived by now.

When I crossed the stage with my degree in English from Ellison-Wright College in Atlanta, Georgia, only Satchel was there to embrace me and celebrate my achievement. It was at that point that I decided I was going to stop dwelling on my parents still being out there. It was also the point at which I realized I was going to move to Port Hilton and try my hand at writing that elusive, literary beast: the Great American Novel.

I was only able to get Satchel to cut me some slack on my decision when I told him I wouldn't buy a house there or lock myself into any long-term agreements that would take away my flexibility. But, I added, if I were to sell a novel to a publisher, all bets were off.

He reluctantly agreed, although we both knew this was a symbolic gesture, as he had no more control over how I used my trust fund than I had over how he used his. The four-year difference in our ages notwithstanding, we were, at this point, two adults.

That's how I eventually came to live at Wingate House on 405 Crestwood Avenue in downtown Port Hilton.

THE HUGE MINT green Victorian looked like some kind of Faulknerian castle, and I would soon learn that it was a failed attempt at a bed and breakfast. As it turns out, Marigold Grant, the owner, could not cook to save her life. She specialized in making food that resembled third grade science projects.

When she took down the bed and breakfast sign and put up a sign saying "Rooms for Rent," she was pleasantly surprised at how quickly tenants lined up. Now she could maintain the house and property while not scaring off tourists with her food.

Of course, all of this happened well before I arrived. Still, two of the original tenants remained: Mr. Golly and Gunther Pratt. I don't know Mr. Golly's first name or even if his name is really Golly. All I know is that's what he wants us to call him and that he uses "golly" as his strongest expletive. Gunther Pratt is a different animal altogether, though. He claims to have been a Black Panther, but says there's no relation to Geronimo. Between the two of these men—and Ms. Grant—gossip runs through them faster than shit through a goose.

That's how I learned, almost three weeks into my stay at Wingate House, that the place was haunted.

I WAS in the heady early days of calling myself a novelist (although I had yet to write a single word), and I welcomed the experience. It would add to my authorial legend, I figured.

"And Hawthorne Caston lived in a haunted Victorian house in Virginia for several years," my future biographer would write.

(In those days my ego was much bigger than it is now. One thing I have learned since I finally completed my novel—and amassed enough rejection letters to plaster half of my room—is that few professions can humble a person as quickly as writing.)

In addition to Ms. Grant, Mr. Golly, and Gunther Pratt, two other people share the house with me: Natalie Pierpont, an upperclassman at the college down the street, and Stephanie Jones, a book sales associate/barista in the town's only bookstore. So as fate would have it, there are three men and three women living separately in this large green house, four black (Mr. Golly, Gunther Pratt, Stephanie, and me) and two white (Ms. Grant and Natalie), and we all get along well—far better than might be expected by some of our Southern counterparts.

Natalie is the person whose age is closest to my own, and while she's cool, my mind is far removed from the days of classes and clubs and homecomings and all the things I bored of while I was still in school. This, though, is less of a condemnation of Natalie and more of a condemnation of my own antisocial ways.

The bottom line is that I was the kind of person who should have never gone to college in the first place. I'm more the autodidactic type, and I tend to overanalyze social activities to the extreme because I've never really felt comfortable around my peers. I just never felt *cool* enough.

Writers don't have to be cool, though—at least cool to anyone other than other writers. Society gives writers a license to be odd ducks, eccentric creatives, detached geniuses, and nongregarious griots. This is clearly my tribe, so while neither Natalie nor Stephanie are bad looking women by a long shot, I don't need the added pressure of liking either of them as more than just housemates.

Natalie moved into the house a month after me, Stephanie a year later. Before that, it was just the four of us: Ms. Grant, Mr. Golly, Gunther Pratt, and me. By then, I already knew many of the secrets of the house for myself: things like the fact that Ms. Grant would always fart loudly early in the morning. It was loud and long, high pitched like a wah-wah guitar being strummed to climax by a bluesman. One long blast, two short blasts, like a train. After the initial shock of the sound, which echoed throughout the wooden house during the early morning hours, and the predictability of its regularity, I came to look at Ms. Grant's farts as a kind of alarm clock or a rooster's cock-a-doodle-doo.

Before I knew it was Ms. Grant, I had assumed it was one of the older men in the house (after all, Mr. Golly enjoyed beans and franks more than any adult male should have), but one morning while heading to the bathroom down the hall, I caught glimpse of Ms. Grant rounding the corner, headed outdoors through the kitchen into the garden, where she did her morning meditation. I distinctly remember her hiking up her leg, ever so slightly, as what sounded like a muted trumpet holding a long, flat note growled throughout the hall. Although I am not a scholar of the morning flatus, I do question whether or not the size of Ms. Grant's rather large bottom impacted the sound—and even length—of her gas. But I digress.

Another secret of the house I came to understand early in my stay is that the house was, in fact, haunted. At first it was Gunther Pratt making occasional comments to Mr. Golly, like, "You can tell she's been angry this week. It's been cold as a witch's tit at night." The kinds of comments he made could have easily been explained away by natural phenomena—definitely nothing supernatural. Mr. Golly would add to the discussion by saying things like, "She just needs to go to the light, is all," as if he were an expert on such matters.

Frankly, I thought both of these men, aged somewhere in their seventies, had lost their marbles a bit, or maybe they had simply grown bored living alone in the rented rooms of an old house and created something to enliven their days a bit more.

But then I saw her for myself.

ۮۑ

ON THE NIGHT I first saw her, I had been out at a sports bar, drinking a few beers and taking in a baseball game that had gone into extra innings. By the time I got home, it was a little after midnight. I was tired, but far from drunk. (I had drunk three beers over the course of five hours, each of them spread out and largely baby-sat until the remainder of the glass grew warm and I ordered another one.) The reason my sobriety is important is because I was unable to use it as an excuse for what I saw.

My key was in the door knob of my room, and I noticed something grayish in my peripheral vision—and it was moving very slowly. I turned my head and saw what was distinctly an apparition floating near the end of the hall.

Part of me wanted to run, but the other part was curious. After all, I'd never seen a ghost (or believed in their existence) and needed time for what rational mind I had to make sense of what I was seeing.

She was definitely a ghost. She appeared to be in her mid-twenties, but because she was dressed in a very rustic-looking dress, I couldn't be sure how accurate I was. She was, however, fairly attractive, something I was surprised Mr. Golly and Gunther Pratt had failed to mention, as they were sometimes prone to wax poetic about various beautiful women from their pasts. This ghost, though, was clearly a young white Southern woman who looked as if she had possibly occupied Wingate House in some capacity other than domestic help.

I had never dated a white woman, but I didn't fear them or the situations that came along with them in Southern culture the way my older housemates did. As I looked upon her slender, floating figure, her hair pulled back into a ponytail that rested between her shoulder blades, I wondered what she might have thought of black people during the time she was alive. The funny thing about ghosts is you have to know exactly when they died, if you can't ascertain that information from simply looking at them. To me, the years before and after the Civil War were wide enough for too many things to be assumed, but if I were to take the most generic assumption of a ghost with her appearance occupying a house like this in Virginia, the former seat of the Confederacy, I would guess that she might have viewed someone like me as property—definitely not her equal.

She turned her head and looked directly at me. For a moment we stared at each other. Her penetrating gaze was surreal, and I felt my knees weaken. I lifted my hand and waved it at her slowly. For a moment, she did nothing but stare, and then without warning, she simply vanished. I think that freaked me out more than anything that had happened up to that point. Maybe it was because I didn't see her actually appear that her disappearance was so jarring. It was as if that action underscored the fact that she was no longer a person after all.

After Natalie and Stephanie moved in, I would still occasionally see the ghost floating through the hall late at night, but I never told anyone. Each time I would wave at her, and shortly after that, she would disappear.

Until one day she didn't.

THINGS GREW INTERESTING around the time I started dating Gargoyle, which you might be surprised to learn is actually a term of endearment for a woman I used to date named Aretha. When I say "Aretha" now, the only thing that comes to mind is the Queen of Soul. That's why I had to give "my" Aretha a nick-name so I could mentally differentiate the two—but I never dared call her "Gargoyle" to her face.

Aretha, with her freckled, light complexion and reddish brown hair pulled back into an Afro bun, would always reciprocate whenever I went down on her, and she did this by kneeling in front of me, her thin arms and narrow shoulders pulled back, almost like wings. She would hold the position until I withered from satisfaction, and her steadfast commitment to this position reminded me of one of the winged statues atop a high-rise. She looked nothing like a gargoyle by the face, but looking at a face in the darkness can play funny tricks on your eyes sometimes.

Anyway, the name stuck—in my head, that is.

Gargoyle liked to wear these wacky t-shirts that played off her name. She once wore a shirt with a joint drawn across it.

"Get it?" she had asked me.

"Get what?"

"My shirt."

"It's a joint," I said.

She smiled, shaking her head. "Try again."

"It's marijuana."

"Again," she said.

"Weed?"

To prevent me from going through the endless nicknames for marijuana, she finally cut me off.

"A reefer! Get it? A reefer. A-retha?"

"Lord, have mercy. You need help."

"Yeah, I do need help—help to some more of that good dick."

T-shirt be damned.

Around the time of our amorous escapades, I started feeling a coolness descend upon us as we slept. It was nothing like a fan or the AC kicking on. It was like someone had left open the door to a deep freezer.

One night as we slept, I distinctly got the feeling we were being watched. When I opened my eyes, though, we were alone, Gargoyle and me, but I knew the ghost had been there.

In the weeks that followed, I got the distinct impression that the ghost did not like the fact that I was spending time with Gargoyle. I could have stopped seeing Gargoyle right then, but, admittedly, I was a bit too sprung on that good-good to do anything too drastic.

Then one night, sweaty and breathless in post-coital bliss, we lay on the bed and the ghost appeared in my bedroom, right next to my bed. She hovered right there, so uncomfortably close. She looked at me as if I had betrayed some unstated trust. All would have been well, except for the fact that Gargoyle awoke to the haunting presence and jumped out of my bed so fast I thought she would sprint through the wall.

"What the fuck?" she yelled, grabbing her things and dashing out of the room at a speed reserved for a gazelle looking to outrun a cheetah.

I had always wondered how my relationship with Gargoyle would end and had assumed either she would find someone with whom she could develop a real relationship or I would. We were placeholders for the other, we knew. What I didn't expect was that the ghost would introduce a third option: Gargoyle would shoot me the deuces, because in her words, "I don't fuck with dead people."

Things settled down after that, and I didn't see the ghost for several days. When she returned to my room, hovering right beside my bed, I waved at her, as had become my custom.

This time she waved back.

Neither of us spoke. We simply looked at each other, first out of curiosity, but after weeks of curiosity, I sensed there was something there—like maybe she wanted something more from me. I couldn't say for sure that I liked her (*could I even like a ghost?*), but I couldn't deny that I would sometimes think of her when I was away from the house. There was something very pretty about her features, and I wondered what she looked like in life, her skin full of color, tangible and soft to the touch. These thoughts eventually took hold of my imagination, and in the absence of a lover, I found myself fantasizing about being with her, the way I would have if she were a living person.

After six months of us staring longingly at each other, our eyes attempting to speak a language our mouths could not yet put into words, I became comfortable with her. Maybe too comfortable, because then I began to get an unsettling feeling. A part of me feared what would happen should I meet someone else, a living person, who piqued my interest.

Somehow, I don't think the ghost would run away like Gargoyle did. Why would she? She belongs to the house.

AT THIS POINT I have probably done very little to dissuade you of my being a little off my rocker, and if that is the case (as it probably is), I can only say that you're probably right after all.

Right now, though, I am staring at the ceiling of my room, as the sun sets just outside my window. The cream colored gritty texture of the ceiling looks a bit like micro stalactites that could break off eventually and cover me in a chalky, dusty cluster of pebbles.

I lie on the bed, wondering if the ghost will come tonight.

"Hawk? You in there?" Stephanie says, knocking on my door.

I slowly sit up and answer, "Yeah."

The door feels like it's a hundred yards away, as my feet trudge slowly, evening fatigue encasing them like dried mud. I open the door, and Stephanie is standing there, her pink horn-rimmed glasses perched on her nose, the walking cliché of a bookseller/barista.

"Are you busy? I mean, I really need your help with something," she says.

"No, I'm cool. What do you need?"

"I need you to go somewhere with me."

"Where?"

"I have a blind date, and I just need you to see his face—just in case he decides to do something stupid."

"Why go out with him if you don't really trust being around him?" I ask.

Stephanie rolls her eyes. "Will you come with me or do I need to ask someone else?"

"It's not a problem. I got you," I respond. There's no point in inquiring further. In this house we carry with us a bit of loneliness, and a blind date is far from the worst remedy for this malady.

We don't speak again until the car is out of the driveway and headed toward Main Street.

"So what's his name?" I ask.

"Barry."

"How did you meet him?"

"We connected online through this website for people who write fan fiction."

"People actually hook up in those places?" I ask.

Stephanie rolls her eyes again. "I knew I should have just waited for Natalie to get home and ask her. You always make fun of us."

"Whoa," I say, surprised. "I don't always make fun of you, and I wasn't making fun of you now. I was just asking a question. My bad. I'll just sit over here and look like the big black man riding in the car with you, so this guy Barry will know not to come at you sideways."

Stephanie pulls over into an empty parking lot.

"Hawk, I'm sorry. I guess I'm just a little uptight. I don't normally do this kind of thing."

"Blind dates with people you meet online?"

"Yeah," she says, putting the car in park.

I look at her, and her face is a mixture of dread and curiosity. "You don't have to go, you know?"

"I can't leave him hanging," she responds.

"This guy could be anybody. He could be catfishing you or something."

"That's why I asked you to come with me," she responds.

I nod. "Okay. But we need a code word, so if this dude is not someone you want to be left alone with, you say the word and we bail on him."

She smiles. "Wingate."

"Wingate? Like our house?"

"Yes."

"Well, Wingate it is."

At this, Stephanie nods enthusiastically. She then shifts the car out of park and continues down the road.

"So where are we meeting him?" I ask.

"At the bookstore."

"You're meeting him at your place where you work?"

She sighs. "I didn't know where else to go. I feel safe there."

"Does he know you work there?" I ask.

"No. It didn't come up."

"That's good. I would hate for him to show up at your job trippin' if this thing went south."

She laughs nervously.

As I look at Stephanie, I realize that she is far prettier than she gives herself credit for. Her skin is a beautiful shade of brown mahogany, and her dark, curly hair radiates outward, almost inviting someone's touch. Even more, she is awkward like me. Maybe in another life I'd have a chance, but in this life, I figure I'm better off as a friend.

"So is he a brother or *another*?" I ask lightly, hoping to make her smile.

"Another," she says, chuckling.

I laugh along with her. I don't know if she has a preference or not, but I figure it's none of my business anyway.

We pull up to the store and park so we can see the cafe area inside. A guy is sitting by the window, his stringy brown hair a bit too long. He looks like the before picture for someone who would go on to become—well, some kind of jackal-beast-man-thing. Even from this distance his acne is pretty strong, and I feel sorry for him. Stephanie is miles outside of his league.

"So that's him?" I ask, looking the guy over. I'm not saying he is *fugly*, but he doesn't favor anyone I've ever seen in my life. My brother is wont to say a guy like Barry was probably hit in the face with a bag of *What the Fuck* at birth, that he was the mold for monster cookies, a guy who fell out of the ugly tree and hit every last branch on the way to the ground, a guy who got beat with the ugly stick like Joe Jackson himself was doing the swinging—but I digress.

"Yep." She takes a breath. "I guess I should go inside and see what he's like."

She starts to open the door, but I reach over and stop her. "I can't let you do that."

She looks at me, her eyes much wider from surprise than I had expected. "Why not?"

"You're too flyy for him. He's way outside his weight class with you."

She pauses. "What are you saying?"

"I'm saying I can't let you go out like that. Can you honestly say that he's the best you can do?"

She lowers her head. "I don't know. He seems interested."

"That's all it takes for you? You should have higher standards."

"Wow," she says, clearly taking offense. "Look who's talking."

"What does that mean?"

She turns her head away from me. "I hear what the old men say. They say you have a thing for some ghost or something. Like you fantasize about being a slave."

I shake my head. This is too much, too fast. I'm trying to digest what she's just said, while at the same time wondering if that's what Mr. Golly and Gunther Pratt really think of me. The gossips have struck again.

Not knowing where to begin, I simply say, "I don't fantasize about being a slave. That's crazy."

She looks at me carefully. "What about the other part? The ghost?"

I look away. I don't know what to say. This is the longest conversation I've ever had with Stephanie, and I'm as uncomfortable as a guy standing in a cathedral during mass, trying to hold in a fart, while he's on the verge of sneezing.

"It's all kind of complicated," I finally say.

She doesn't appear at all fazed by this admission. "Well, I'm going to go and see if I have anything in common with this guy. So if you don't mind hanging back and keeping an eye on us, I'd really appreciate it."

She reaches for the door handle and I place a hand on her shoulder. "Are you sure about this? You could do so much better."

"Ha!" she says mockingly. "I guess you could, too."

As she opens the door, I say, "Then let's do better."

"What does that mean?"

"I mean, we can both hold out for something better. I'm prepared to do that, if you are."

She looks at the guy in the cafe. He's fidgeting with his

phone, and I can't help wondering when he last bathed. "I should at least go and tell him that I'm not interested."

I shake my head back and forth rapidly, my cheeks slapping against my teeth. "Nope. Hard pass. Just message him later and say something came up and you couldn't make it. After that, just ghost him—no pun intended." I pause because she is laughing again. "Ignore his messages. I'm serious. Does he even know what you look like?"

"He knows I'm black. That's about it."

"How in the world did you manage that in the age of the Internet?"

She smiles. "I don't use real photos for my avatars, and I don't use my name either."

"Smart," I offer.

"So. Now what?"

"You hungry?" I ask.

"Sure."

"Let's go get a bite to eat and just hang out for a bit."

She looks at the guy again and then sits back and fastens her seatbelt. She places her hands on the steering wheel as she weighs whether she will actually jilt this dude. She exhales and finally says, "Okay."

⚜

STEPHANIE POKES at what's left of her French fries. I can tell she is still bothered about standing up Barry. I know in my gut I should be stepping up to the plate here. It's not like Stephanie isn't finer than frog hair, but I think about the logistics of dating someone who lives in the same house with me—and then there's, of course, the ghost.

Still, she looks so lonely sitting over there, as if doing the right thing were the same as doing the hardest thing.

I decide to say some off-hand shit. "You're not attracted to me, are you? I mean, I don't want to make you uncomfortable by stepping to you or anything."

Not only is this one of the wackest things I have ever said, but it was totally unnecessary and apropos of absolutely nothing.

I quickly back-step. "You don't have to answer that. I'm tripping. I'm nervous. Let me shut up before I say something else stupid."

She starts chuckling, and I realize that I have found a new favorite thing. I would give up writing and become a comedian if I could have her laughing like that on the regular.

She picks up one of her French fries and waves it at me like a wand. I immediately feel the weight of the world lifting from my shoulders. "You're crazy, you know," she says, taking a bite.

"Yeah. I pretty much am."

After that, the conversation loosens. Laughter as a laxative, I figure.

"So there's really a ghost in our house?" she asks.

I nod. "I couldn't believe it either."

"And you and the ghost...you know?"

I shrug my shoulders, no longer embarrassed by the idea of it. "She just comes into my room and watches me, and I watch her back. We have an understanding."

"Is she white?"

"Actually she's gray."

"You know what I mean," she says, chuckling again.

"Yeah, she's white. My guess is that she never married and was living in the house when she died. I think she was in her twenties."

Stephanie takes another bite of her fries. "I'm actually surprised you never asked."

"I don't think she can talk. And to be honest, I never got around to playing charades with her to figure that part out."

She nods and takes a sip of her drink. "How much longer do you plan to stay in the house?"

I shrug. "You?"

"It's about all I can afford—at least for the moment."

I nod. "I feel you."

We sit a while longer, listening to the random music coming from the diner's jukebox, before rising to leave.

"I know it wasn't a date with Ol' Yuck-ney of His Mother's Basement, but I hope I wasn't a complete waste of time."

She laughs again, and I pat myself on the back for batting 1.000.

"I had fun. A lot of fun," she responds, as we head back to her car.

"You know, we should really have taken my car," I say.

"But I'm the one who invited you to come with *me*."

"Still, if I were to be the proper chaperone, I should have at least been behind the wheel."

"Well, maybe next time," she says.

"Really? Would you like to go out again?"

"What exactly are you asking me?"

I pause for a moment. "I had a good time with you. If you're down, maybe we can hang out again."

"Hang out."

"Hang out, unless you know you might be feeling a brother, you know?" I am just unable to stop the corny shit from pouring from my lips.

"That's the second time you've put it out there. I guess I should be asking if you're 'feeling a sister,' since you're over there cracking jokes."

I look at her and in that moment I can't tell if she wants me to make a move or if she's just trying to make sense of me so she can know how to handle me going forward, platonically.

"You're a beautiful woman. That's all I'm saying."

"That's all you're saying?"

"Well, I could say more, but I don't want to make you feel a way about all of this."

She considers this and says, "What if I told you I thought you were handsome?"

"Don't play with me," I say. "I don't want to be out here dancing in the parking lot for no damn reason."

She laughs.

"You a'ight," she says, smiling.

I feel my heart beating rapidly, and I want to say something really smooth. Instead, I open the driver's door for her and walk around to the passenger side.

"You a'ight, too," I respond.

She starts up the car, and I look out the window, my mind racing with questions, but anchored in place by the feeling that comes from the satisfaction of mutual affection.

৩৯৫৩

WE HUG in the car before we head to our rooms, content to keep our outing a secret. When I reach my room and lie down on the bed, I feel the temperature around me drop. I sit up in the darkness and see the ghost hovering beside me. Her arms are crossed, and while I hadn't shown any sign of affection toward Stephanie in the house, the ghost apparently has a sixth sense (pun intended) like many women who can sense their men have been out with other women. She genuinely looks both sad and disappointed in me.

"Hey," I say. "I was just out with a friend. Just being friendly."

Even as I hear my own voice and the repetition of the word "friend," I know I have already tipped my hand. I am clearly interested in someone else, as far as the ghost is concerned.

"I don't know what to say," I finally offer. "You and I can't talk to each other. I don't even know what *this* is or how you feel. You're a ghost, for crying out loud! Where can all of this go?"

As I wait for her to offer some type of communication, she points at me, almost like a warning, and then she disappears!

Although I have seen her disappear before, this time it scares the shit out of me (two drops of pee, I tell you). It felt like she was giving me a warning.

I start to pull the covers in my bed over my head, but figure what's the point? There is nothing in this house that I can outrun anyway.

҈

I HOP out of bed when I hear Ms. Grant's morning fart. It's early, and I know she's headed outside to meditate. I wait a few minutes so that (1) I don't startle her, and (2) the fart dissipates and I don't torture myself unnecessarily walking through the hall. When I see her behind the house, she is stretching on a mat staring into the trees that separate her property from the neighbor's.

I clear my throat so she's aware of my presence. I just figure it's good etiquette not to surprise an elderly white woman during the quiet hours of the morning, even if she's one of the coolest people in Port Hilton.

She turns to face me. "Hawthorne? What are you doing up this early?"

"Just came outside for some fresh air." I smile to myself at the cleverness of this remark, especially after I had just navigated the flatus battlefield only moments earlier.

"I like to come out here in the morning and get my head clear for the rest of the day," she says.

"It's definitely nice out here," I offer.

A beat passes and Ms. Grant resumes her stretching. "What can I do for you?"

Not wanting to interrupt her routine any more than necessary, I say, "What can you tell me about the ghost in our house?"

She laughs abruptly and a little gas pops out with each exhalation. "Sorry. Wow, that's embarrassing. At my age, though, you can celebrate the fact that it's just a little gas and not more." She laughs again, this time without the punctuation of gas.

I dig the fact that Ms. Grant just doesn't give a fuck. From the time that I have known her, she has lived a life of few regrets —as far as I can tell. I seriously believe she monitors her actions based on whether or not she causes harm to others. That's a dope mantra to live by, if you ask me.

"The ghost?" I say, in an effort to refresh her memory and not take a tangent.

"You know how to ask a loaded question early in the morning, don't you?" She stretches a bit more then takes a seat on the mat. She invites me to sit down next to her.

She turns to face me and says, "I bought this house thirty years ago. I had to fix it up and that took a while, especially when my husband passed on. We never had any children, so I was pretty lonely when he died. And I had this huge house. I didn't know what to do. Then one day I got the idea to start a bed and breakfast, and well, that was another misstep. I always knew I wasn't much of a cook, but I didn't know what else to do with a house this big and keep up the mortgage payments. I lucked up on the renting situation. I guess that was Arthur's way of saying, 'Honey, I'm going to nudge you in the right direction so you don't lose this house.'"

I nod. "Arthur? That's your late husband?"

"Yep. But to get back to your question about the ghost. I guess I knew when we bought the house, but because of how old the structure is, the realtor didn't bother with the distressed property component. I guess when you think of it, most of the places in the world are the locations of somebody's death, whether there's a building there or not."

I nod again. "Did you ever try to find out anything about the people who lived here in the past?"

Ms. Grant looks out at the trees again. "I did a little poking around—especially after I saw the woman floating in the hall."

My eyes grow wider. "That's her. I see her often." I don't add on the other part of that equation.

"I believe her name is Martha Wingate. She was the only child of a local judge. She never married and supposedly died of tuberculosis in her mid-twenties."

"About how long ago was this?"

"She died in the early 1870's, I believe."

"So her parents owned slaves?"

"Hawthorne, I don't know. This area became a safe haven for runaway slaves toward the end of the Civil War, from what I've read. I haven't come across anything to point to which side the Wingates might have sided with."

"You really know a lot about this stuff," I say.

"Well, when you have a huge house and time on your hands, you can learn a lot of things."

"Yeah. I suppose you're right."

She starts to stand again, stretching her legs. "So why all the questions—especially now? You've lived here for a while now. You're just now getting curious about this?"

"I guess I just wanted to know the full story."

"No problem. If this stuff scares you and you decide to leave, keep in mind I need at least a sixty day notice of your intent to vacate the premises." She smiles at me, but I know she's serious.

"Thanks. I'll let you get back to your meditating."

"All right. Take care."

I walk back to the house, and as I close the door, I hear a ripple of gas out in the distance.

☙❧

STILL ON EDGE from my last encounter with Martha, I decide to go *incognegro* with my feelings for Stephanie. We take to texting each other, but she believes this is our rudimentary attempt at keeping our bubbling interest under wraps from the rest of the house—although I suspect Natalie has already been put in the loop, as the two of them were already pretty close. The truth, though, is that I don't know what Martha would do, should she find out any more than what she already seems to know. I keep having flashbacks to Gargoyle running out of the house, and I know in my gut that what Stephanie and I could have is much more meaningful and therefore cannot be subject to the same outcome.

Our second date takes place at a park on the edge of town, far enough away from the house that neither of us feels the added pressure. The sun is setting just beyond the bay, extending into the horizon. Stephanie reaches into a basket she has brought along and pulls out the turkey and cheese sandwiches she's made for us, along with a bag of chips and two bottles of water. It's a simple picnic, but I'm still abuzz with the feeling that she would go through any trouble for me, especially taking it upon herself to feed me.

"The food looks wonderful," I say. To me the sandwich may as well be filet mignon and the water, wine. Her presence has elevated the meal to four-star quality.

"Thank you," she says, taking a bite.

I join her, as we eat our sandwiches in silence, our eyes cast upon the pinkish hue of the sky.

When we finish, she asks, "So how is your novel coming?"

I smile. "Frankly, it's one meandering mess. I don't know if I should start over or look into some workshops where I can get some feedback on how to fix it."

"I'd be happy to read it," she offers.

"I'm tempted. Maybe you *could* fix it. Still, I don't really know how bad it is. I've been rejected nearly a hundred times, I shit you not. All of those agents and editors can't be wrong. Can they?"

Stephanie shrugs her shoulders. "Who knows? But I know this: a lot of books made their way into the world with more rejections than yours."

"Well, if you want to read it, I can definitely email you a copy tonight."

"Thanks."

I look down at her hands, her long slender fingers and polish-free nails, and raise my gaze to her wrists, then up her arm. At that moment I want only to be touched by her, to feel those fingers interlocked with my own. I now see why I had avoided even paying too much attention to her. I was afraid that I would be in a moment like this with her one day, wanting to kiss her but not having the courage to make that move.

"I really like you," I say. This small declaration takes more courage than I'm willing to admit.

She looks at me and then removes her glasses. Seeing her eyes hypnotizes me, and I am reminded of what Jamie Foxx said about meeting Prince for the first time. I guess some people have the ability to win you over completely with their eyes. I remember Barry back at the bookstore and realize that, like him, I might be entirely out of my league with Stephanie.

"I like you, too," she finally says. "The other night when we got back from the restaurant I couldn't stop thinking about you."

"Really? I thought it was just me."

She places her hand on mine and I feel a tingle shoot

through all of my fingers at once. At that moment I want to kiss her like nobody's business. My stomach is churning with a factory of butterflies, and I feel as if anxiety has been painted over my body like a thick, sticky, immobilizing film. But the kiss is there for the taking, I tell myself, as our eyes lock, our lips full and expectant. I tell myself that I will count down from five and make my move.

Five.

Four.

Three.

Two.

One.

And I lean in.

Stephanie leans in to meet me.

❧

WHILE WE LEFT our passions only upon our lips, that does not quell the lust that burns there as I now stare at my ceiling, replaying those moments with Stephanie. I knew I wanted more —still want more—but there is something beautiful, simple, and pure in what we experienced in our first moment of intimacy. There will be plenty of time for us to explore even more of each other.

My body feels warm beneath the covers, hungry and yearning, and when I close my eyes, I easily drift off to sleep.

❧

I OPEN my eyes to find the room feels like an icebox. Turning my head, I see that someone is lying in bed next to me. Her hair is brownish blonde from what I can make out in the moonlight trickling through the blinds. I can feel the weight of her cool body right next to me. I immediately know who it is, but I am afraid to touch her.

She begins to turn around, rolling herself over slowly. I want to turn my face away or run, but I realize both notions are futile. When her face comes into view, I am struck by just how beautiful Martha really is. She looks at me and smiles. I reluctantly smile back.

"Do you love me?" she asks. Her voice is hollow, there but not there. It's almost as if I can perceive her voice rather than hear it.

I don't know how to respond to her. It's not that I don't know the answer, but I'm afraid of saying something unrequited to a person who is not alive. She senses my hesitation, and her eyebrows furrow. She is pretty even when she is upset.

She then places an ice cold hand on my arm, the feeling so cold that it feels like it's burning my skin. Then she smiles so widely that her face flips open upon itself in a grotesque balloon of bone and muscle. I scream and close my eyes.

Moments later I am shaken awake by Stephanie, whose concern brings me back into reality.

"Are you all right?" she asks.

"The ghost…" is all I can manage.

I rub my arm where Martha touched me.

"What happened right there?" Stephanie asks, pointing to my arm.

Even in the semi-darkness of the room, I can see a dark hand-like print on my arm, my skin darkened and debossed.

"I think she's angry," I say.

Thinking that Stephanie will take off running, just like Gargoyle did, I am pleasantly surprised when she pulls me warmly into her embrace and holds me until I can feel myself again.

THE FACT that I had to be comforted by Stephanie in the middle of the night does not go unnoticed by Gunther Pratt and Mr. Golly when I see them the next morning sitting on the porch.

"Golly gee," Mr. Golly says. "You something else!"

I shrug my shoulders, not completely sure what he means. I look to Gunther Pratt for an explanation, but he is gobbling a handful of strawberries from his palm and coughing the whole time.

He clears his throat a few times and says, "My thoat stratchy as hell from these gottdamn scrawberries."

"Why you keep eatin' 'em then?" Mr. Golly asks.

"'Cause I love scrawberries. That's why."

Mr. Golly points at me, like he's trying to remember my name, and says, "This one here trying to wet his beak at the house. Golly!"

Gunther Pratt lifts his head from his palm and stares at me, sizing me up. "You ain't supposed to shit where you eat," he says, before sticking his pinky finger in his ear and squealing to clear his throat.

I know what he's getting at, although it takes me a second to decode his language. The two of them are essentially warning me about the dangers of dating someone you live in the same house with. I can see their argument clearly, as I have long held the same notion, but now things seem different, and I want the chance to see where things go with Stephanie. Our living under the same roof is a minor inconvenience, as far as I'm concerned.

"You ain't still humpin' that haint, is you?" Gunther Pratt asks, his voice still raspy.

"What are you talking about?" I ask, not at all incredulous. I really have no idea of what he's talking about.

"That ghost? You still messing 'round with that ghost?"

"Huh?" I respond. It's the only thing I can think to say. I figure if I act like I don't understand the question, the question will disappear.

Mr. Golly leans toward me. "He wants to know if you is trying to intercourse that dead white girl." He says this to me like I have a limited understanding of English.

I smile and respond, "I'm just doing me. I don't belong to anybody." It's a weak response and one clearly aimed at appealing to the bravado so often celebrated by older Black men.

"Well, just be careful is all I'm sayin'," Gunther Pratt says. "When them haints get up on you, they don't likes to let go."

I nod, considering for the first time whether he actually has a point that I need to ponder. Do I really think that she will leave me alone so I can pursue a real relationship with a real person? I want to believe that this is anything other than a love triangle. That doesn't even make sense.

I nod my farewell to the men and head to my car. I have no idea where I am going to go, but I know that I need to get away from the house.

❧

"It's called Haint Blue," Satchel says over my car speakers, as if he just revealed the most obvious thing in the world to me. My brother can be a bit of an ass sometimes.

The Blue-Tooth-connected microphone is situated just above my head in the roof of the car, and I'm careful not to sigh loud enough for him to hear me.

"So tell me about this Haint Blue stuff," I finally say.

"It's like a blueish green, turquoise-kind of color that looks like green ocean foam. They sell it in just about every paint shop, especially ones in The South."

"And what do you do with it?" I ask.

"Most people paint the underpart of the ceiling over the porch of their house. That's supposed to help keep the ghosts away. The problem with you, though, is that the ghost is already in the house." He says this last part, barely able to conceal his laughter. It's all right that he doesn't believe me. The information is far more important than my pride at this point.

I had broken down and reached out to Satchel when I couldn't think of anyone else to talk to about this stuff. I knew he would hear me out, even if he ridiculed me in the process. If he wasn't such an ass with me, I'd probably worry that something was wrong—and frankly I don't need the added stress of having to worry about him alongside this other shit I'm already dealing with.

"I guess I can talk to Ms. Grant about painting the ceiling in my room. Maybe that will push the ghost out and give me more privacy."

"Yeah, that, or you could just move to another place. I've been telling you that you can do better than living in some old house with a bunch of people. You act like you're not sitting on a million."

"That's not me," I remind him, relieved that he's finally easing up on how I spend my money. "I just want to focus on my writing, and being in an environment like this feels good for me."

"Little brother, check this. People write novels in coffee shops, in libraries, in bookstores, at home. I'm pretty sure some people are writing them on their cell phones at this point. You can't tell me that being in a house like that—with a damn ghost —is the best thing for your writing, can you?"

I sigh. I know what Satchel wants me to say, but I won't give him that luxury. "I'm going to do my best to make it work."

I thank him and tell him that I'm going to pick up the paint, before hustling to get off the phone.

Haint blue? Could my problems really be solved by a coat of paint?

Ms. Grant doesn't immediately take to my suggestion about the blue paint. At first I fear that she might look at the idea as being overly superstitious, but then she tells me that she worries that the ghost might actually be offended by the proposed change. It is at this point that I am forced to tell her a few more details about my involvement with our resident spirit.

She eyes me suspiciously. "Are you telling me the truth, Hawthorne?" she asks, unsure if what I am saying is really any more absurd than what she already knows to be true about the house.

"Yes. I've been romantically involved with the ghost of Martha Wingate. But now things have changed, and there's someone new in my life. Someone who is actually living."

She shakes her head, as if doing this will settle her thoughts. "Assuming I buy into what you're telling me, you think painting the ceilings will keep her from going rogue on us?"

I then recount my experience with the ghost in my bed, a situation I still haven't completely contextualized as real, although I am not above forgiving myself for using this anecdote, sans any veracity. By the time I complete my story, I have painted the portrait of a ghost that is angry enough to do some real haunting, and not just "floating around in the halls" kind of stuff.

What neither Ms. Grant nor I say is that I could simply move from the house, just like Satchel suggested. But I pay rent on a distressed property (and I pay that rent on time), so Ms. Grant will at least hear me out. Outside of that, I like the house in general, and not because of my writer fantasies. At this point in my life, I feel conditioned to be in this environment, and without my parents around and my brother in an entirely different state, I feel like being in this house, with these people, keeps me from feeling lonely about my life.

"Okay," Ms. Grant finally says. "If you're going to buy the paint, you may as well paint over the porch and through the first floor hall, and get the shutters as well."

I know better than to complain about the extra paint and extra work, so I nod my thanks and head over to one of the local hardware stores to buy everything I will need.

❧

THE ASSOCIATE WORKING the paint section has more questions than I am prepared to answer.

"There're 'bout a dozen haint blue shades out there. Which 'un you lookin' for?"

"Is there a Virginia shade?" I ask.

He scans through the paint labels on the various brands that are in the general color range. "Nope. We got Savannah, Ohio, Charleston, and a *lah mason.*"

I note the "La Maison" name but don't bother correcting him. "I'll take a blend of the four then."

"Well, damn," he responds, staring at the computer screen.

"What's wrong?"

"Well, uh, we mix each of the paint colors in the store, percentages and whatnot. This amount of blue, this amount of white, this amount of yellow. Now I gots to mix four different paints and then mix all of them together. You tryin' to buy all these cans or do I need to break out my calculator?"

"No problem," I respond, just to keep the peace, plus you never know how much paint you might need down the road. "I'll buy it all."

The guy smiles, revealing a wide gap between his front teeth. "I'll get right to it then."

By the time I leave the store with my Franken-paint and supplies, I am ready to get down to business.

I figure I'll start in my bedroom, since that's the place that, at this point, concerns me most.

৩৯৩

Once I finish placing the paint in the trunk of my car, my phone vibrates, indicating that I've received a text message.

Is everything okay? Ms. Grant said that you're gonna be doing some painting in the hallway.

I'm relieved to see Stephanie's message. I text her back with an update of how I am hoping the paint will rid us of the ghost.

Well, let me know if you need any help, she texts.

Normally I would welcome all the help I can get, but this time I tell her I will take care of it alone. After all, this is a problem I created for myself. If I could get myself into it, then I have to believe I can get myself out of it.

When I reach 405 Crestwood Avenue, I throw a plastic tarp over the furniture in my room and place plastic down on the floor. I pull out the small ladder I bought and climb to the penultimate step, paintbrush in hand. It is only after I have painted a large swath of the ceiling that I realize that I will have to check into a hotel room for the night. It was a simple thing to include in my preparations, but in my quest to get ahead of Martha with the haint blue, I allowed the basic logistics of painting a room to completely disappear from my thoughts. I would only need to stay in a hotel room overnight, and I figured I would leave the overhead fan running and crack the windows slightly to expedite the drying time.

Once I finish the room, I wash up and pack a small overnight bag. I will deal with painting the other parts of the house tomorrow. Right now, I just want to get checked in and kick back and relax.

"Where are you going?" Stephanie asks, as she sees me walking out into the hall with my bag.

"I just finished painting my ceiling, and I have to rent a hotel room to sleep in overnight while the paint dries."

"Oh."

I observe her reaction of mild disappointment. "What are you up to?"

She shrugs her shoulders. "I'm off today. Just sitting around the house, trying to get into this new book, but it's a slow process."

"Well, you're welcome to come with me," I respond. I don't know where these words come from or what has given me the audacity to ask her to spend the night with me. But lately things have been completely unpredictable, and I figure the worst she could do is decline my invitation. Hell, we're grown and we like each other. It's not that ridiculous an invitation.

"I'd like that." She smiles at me in a way that makes my breath quicken. I can hear my brother's voice toying with me. *Aw sookie sookie now! Shit is real, kid!* She holds up a finger and says, "Give me a minute to put together an overnight bag."

When she goes back into her room, I try to steel my thoughts. I haven't been with a woman since Gargoyle. But this also feels differently. I didn't have serious feelings for Aretha, but I do have them for Stephanie. That makes all of this much more intense for me.

Stephanie meets me at my car fifteen minutes later. By this time, I have reserved a room at the Port Hilton Inn across town. I take in her beauty as she walks down the steps from the porch, her beautiful brown skin reflecting the sunlight of the fall afternoon. Her hair is pulled back into a curly bun, and her glasses give her the appearance of a woman I could see myself waking up to every day of the year.

"I'm ready," she says, holding a large red backpack in front of her.

The words ring in my head as we turn out of the driveway.

☙❧

"So I guess everyone knows now," I say.

She smiles and offers a slight shrug. "I guess so."

"Does that mean we're a couple?" The question hangs out there for a moment. I haven't had an actual girlfriend in years, and it feels awkward thinking of myself as someone's boyfriend. Even the word *boyfriend* seems like it was intended for kids, not grown-ups.

"I don't know," she responds. "What do you want us to be?"

"I just want to be with you."

"And I want to be with you, too."

Searching for the words, I take a deep breath.

She looks at me, and I try not to wilt under her stare. I know I need to say something, but I'm so rusty at this I don't know how to ask a simple question that she has every right to hear me ask. Finally, I say, "Do you want to be exclusive?" In my head that sounds better than asking her be my girlfriend, where the checking of boxes on notebook paper would be more appropriate.

"I'd like that very much ," she responds, smiling.

My hand loosens on the steering wheel, and it is only then that I realize I have been squeezing it, my perspiration slicking up the vinyl. The clamminess of my hands keeps me from reaching out to hold her hand. Instead, I offer her the smile I am unable to contain.

Once we get checked into the room, the situation really

begins to take hold of me. We're a couple and we will be spending the night together. Maybe it's the newness of it all or just the fact I am allowing myself to be emotionally available for the first time in years that makes all of this feel brand new. As if on cue, the butterflies come back to remind me I have taken the first step toward something that can wind up being the real deal.

⚜

"Okay," Stephanie says. "I have one for you. What's your favorite Prince song?"

We are lying across the bed, side by side, staring up at the ceiling. The only light comes from a small lamp near the door, and it casts just enough light that we can make out each other. Our shadows hover against the wall, on top of the other, a type of foreshadowing that rests throughout the air of the room.

"'Computer Blue.'"

"Really? He hardly sings on that one."

"Well," I say, "you must be one of those fans who swears by 'Adore' or 'Insatiable' or something like that."

She nudges me playfully. "Actually, my favorite Prince song is 'U Got the Look.'"

"Huh? Are you serious? The duet with Sheena Easton? That's your favorite Prince song?"

"Wow. Shade," she responds, her smile broad and beautiful.

"It's dope—don't get me wrong—but it wouldn't make my top twenty-five for Prince songs."

"And more shade."

"Help me understand," I say.

She turns over on her stomach and crosses her legs, propping herself up on her elbows. "Do you remember the whole *Sign O' the Times* tour? That was a few years after *Purple Rain*."

"Not really, but I saw the video for the song."

"Well, the video had the feel of the tour. The song is simple, I'll give you that. Basic blues chord structure, but it kicks you hard in your face. Plus, Prince had the dopest stage entourage ever! Shelia E. Cat Glover. Oh my god. I wanted a body like Cat! Everything about the video and the song are just sexy as hell."

I nod. "So the video is what makes the song work for you?"

"I don't see how you could separate the two."

I shrug. "You might have a point. Back in the 80s and 90s Prince was sex on a stick anyway. Ass cheeks out. Hips exposed. And he had the baddest women in music in his band."

She takes my hand playfully, interlocking my fingers with hers. "Videos matter, like Black lives," she says, smiling.

"Okay, Miss Childish Gambino."

"If you really think about it, for 'Computer Blue' to be your favorite Prince song, you probably experienced it first from watching *Purple Rain*. Even then, he was playing with his shirt off, milking the sex out of the song with Wendy's guitar fellatio." She massages my hand and winks.

"You might have a point," I respond, turning to face her. "Fellatio? That's an interesting word."

Our lips meet immediately, tired of the back and forth, the delay, the stalling. And when her body enters my embrace, I get a glimpse of how beautiful our future will be.

෧෨

WE HARDLY GET ANY SLEEP. It's only after we shower together that our bodies begin to show signs of fatigue. I call for an hour extension on the checkout time, realizing we will not use any of that remaining time for sleeping.

When we finally leave the hotel, we head next door to Cracker Barrel and have a hearty breakfast. By the time we get back in the car, Stephanie is fast asleep. She is sleeping so hard her mouth is open, and I can hear the soft sounds of her snoring. I smile, wishing I could be asleep, too. Instead, I have to wait roughly fifteen minutes before I can get into my bed and stretch out completely.

The drive across Port Hilton is quiet and picturesque, a collage of older and newer homes seated in the shade of large trees. Occasionally I glance over at Stephanie sleeping. *She's my girl*, I think to myself, trying out the words in my head.

I nod my head rhythmically, suddenly aware of the soft music playing through the car speakers. Brandy's "Put That On Everything" frames the image of Stephanie into the soundtrack of my memory. I remember the feel of her hands touching me, holding me, embracing me. My lips tingle at the thought of her kisses. I can even feel the faint traces of her moistness enveloping me during her sensual movements. She stirs in her sleep, and I pray at that moment she is reliving the last eighteen hours in her head, as well.

We pull up to the house and I half-expect to see Mr. Golly and Gunther Pratt out on the porch playing checkers, but I don't see them—or anyone for that matter. A wave of relief flows over me. I wasn't ready to deal with the old men asking questions about Stephanie and me—not yet.

I tap her leg lightly and lean over, kissing her cheek. "Hey, Steph. We're here. Back at the house."

It takes me nudging her a few times before she finally opens her eyes and stretches her arms. "Hey, you," she says, her voice low and sexy, the kind of raspy that only comes with hours of sex and the accompanying sleep deprivation.

"We're home," I say, reaching for her hand and squeezing it gently.

She stretches again and then reaches down between her ankles and grabs her backpack. "Well, I guess I should get some sleep.

You're welcome to come to my room," she says, "but I probably won't be any good for a few hours."

I smile. "Get you some sleep. I'll check in with you a little later. Plus, I still have to paint the hall and the area above the porch."

"Be sure to get some rest before you start working. I don't want you climbing any ladders or anything until you're rested. Promise me that, okay?"

Her concern is flattering. I nod my consent.

She leans over and kisses me, then steps out of the car with her bag and walks into the house. I watch her walk away, and again I am struck by how fine she is.

I grab my bag out the backseat. The only thing I want to do is fall asleep, but when I reach the porch, I realize that something is a bit off. I just can't tell what.

I place my bag down on the porch, twist the knob on the front door, and step across the threshold. It is at that point I realize something is terribly wrong.

჻

THE FIRST THING I notice is that all of the objects in the entire house are laid out differently. The overhead lights are gone. The curtains are drawn and the room is filled with natural light. All of the furniture looks antique, like it was acquired from someone at great expense.

I begin to walk toward my room, and by this time, I am convinced someone is playing a trick on me. I have no idea of what anyone would gain from doing this, but the quaintness of the place brings out the true character of the house, so I decide to ride with it a little longer.

When I reach my room, I turn the knob, but it won't budge. I reach in my pocket to remove my key, but when I search for the key hole, it's not there. In its place is a slot for what I imagine is a skeleton key. *Ms. Grant is really taking this thing kind of far*, I think, jiggling the doorknob again. I scan my mind to remember if I'm paid up on my rent (I am) or if there is something else that would have caused her to lock me out of my room.

When I realize that I'm at a loss for what's happening, I walk upstairs to see if Ms. Grant is in her room. The warmth hanging in the air is only tempered by the windows being open in an effort to catch whatever shaded breeze can slide into the house. It is even more antiquated up here.

"Ms. Grant!" I call out. "Ms. Grant!"

No one answers, and for the first time I consider that I might actually be in the wrong house.

I jog downstairs, my bag hooked around my shoulder, and walk toward the entrance. If this is a different house, it has the exact same layout as 405 Crestwood. This realization causes me to pause.

What the hell is going on?

I reach for the knob on the front door and quickly realize that it's different, more ornate and without a keyhole. I open it and my heart nearly leaps out of my chest. There is nothing there! Blackness as far as the eye can see, just outside the front door, where the porch used to be.

I quickly close the door and step back. When I turn around, I see that it has suddenly become dark in the house, and lamps along the house, interspersed with candlelight, cast unfamiliar shadows against the walls. Not even five minutes earlier, it was clearly daytime, right before noon. Now it looks like it's late evening.

Knowing that I want no parts of what lies outside the front door, I walk back into the house. I reach in my pocket and pull out my iPhone, but it won't start. The battery is dead. It's just a sleek black brick in my hand—useless.

"Stephanie!" I call out. "Stephanie, are you here?"

I stand still and listen as hard as I can. I am met with silence. I know I just saw her walk into this house a few minutes before me. Surely she can't have just disappeared.

"Stephanie!" I say again, my voice as loud as I can make it. It's the kind of voice I would have never used in the house, with the acoustics here, but I am desperate now.

When she doesn't answer, I realize I am on my own, and all I want to do is get back to something I recognize.

As I move through the foyer, I can suddenly hear the murmur of what sounds like voices coming from somewhere down the hall. A feeling of relief washes over me when I realize I am not alone.

When I get closer, I can make out what sounds like a group of people arguing. The closer I get, the more I hear.

"So this is the nigger?" an older man says.

"This is him," another man responds.

"Daddy, please!" This voice is a woman's.

"Sir, I love her," another male voice says.

"Nigger, you don't speak in this house. You hear me?" the older voice responds.

"Daddy, please!" the woman says again, her voice emphatic. "I love him, too."

"Roosevelt," the older man says. "I don't want to see this nigger again. Get him out of my sight."

"Sure thing, Judge Wingate," Roosevelt responds. "I got some of the fellas meeting me over at Jeb Tyler's property. We'll take care of this 'un tonight."

"Daddy!"

"Martha, it's okay. They can't make me stop loving you," the other male voice says.

"You black son of a bitch! If you say one more word in my

house, I will shoot you in your nigger face!" Judge Wingate says. "Roosevelt, get this animal out of my house!"

When I hear them exiting the study, I try to hide in one of the side rooms, but I am not quick enough. Roosevelt leaves the room, his gloved hand gripping the arm of a black man whose wrists are bound together. The black man's face is battered, bleeding, but beneath the swelling I see his face looks nearly identical to my own. Neither of them see me. It's as if I am not there. I reach out to choke the shit out Roosevelt and help out the brother, but my hand goes right through him, as if he is an apparition!

The woman starts to exit the room, and right before she is snatched back into the room by whom I think is Judge Wingate, I see that it is Martha.

I hear Roosevelt and the battered guy head out the front door, and I chase out after them, hoping to be able to exit this ghost house, too.

When I get there I am met only with the endless blackness I saw before.

❧❧❧

I HAVE no idea of how long I have been standing in the foyer of this house. I am trapped and fear that I will never get back to the present.

Then I hear the whisking sound of a dress moving briefly down the hall from the study. It must be Martha.

I rush out into the hall and begin to follow her down the hall. Maybe she knows how to release me from this. She walks down the hall to my bedroom, and just as she opens the door, she turns back to look at the study behind me. Then she stares directly at me.

Can she see me? I wonder. Maybe she is looking through me, past me.

I lift my hand and wave at her.

She lifts her hand and waves back, shock in her tear-filled eyes.

She ventures closer and looks at me.

"Can you hear me?" I ask.

"Are you saying something?" she whispers to me, as she leans in closer to me. She coughs really hard before examining me. "Johnathan, is that you?"

"No," I say, shaking my head. "I'm Hawk."

"I can't hear what you're saying," she says, her gaze full of curiosity. "Look at what you're wearing. And what is that thing you're carrying on your shoulder?" She coughs again, the power of it shaking her body.

I remove the book bag and set it down in front of me. "Help," I mouth. "Please help me!"

Just then, Judge Wingate storms down the house and actually walks right through me! He grabs Martha's arm roughly and pushes her into the bedroom, locking the door with a skeleton key he produces from his pocket. He continues on upstairs to the second floor.

I need to get out of here! I run back to the front door. I open it and stare into the blackness. At this point I do not care anymore. I count down from five and leap into the darkness.

I LAND ON THE GROUND—*HARD*.

The sunlight is blinding, and I have to shield my eyes for a moment.

"That was the craziest shit I ever did see," Gunther Pratt says.

"I done seen kids jump off porches before, but you a grown-ass man. And you dived off that bitch like you was Michael Phelps!"

I laugh, just glad to be back in the present.

"Golly, you a'ight?" Mr. Golly asks.

"Pretty good," I answer.

"I don't even wanna know what was goin' through yo goddamn head," Gunther Pratt adds. "Humpin' them damn haints done got you all discombobulated and shit, I see."

"No. No haints for me," I respond, standing and dusting myself off.

Then I remember that Stephanie is in the house. I run inside, and when I find her, I hold on to her like there's no tomorrow.

⚜

WHEN I FINALLY AWAKE FROM the coma of fatigue that followed me home from the Port Hilton Inn, I replay what happened to me when Stephanie and I returned from the hotel. How the hell did I wind up in the 1800s? This question bothered me for a while. I refused to get out of bed until I could halfway wrap my mind around what happened. I had to figure it out so I didn't wind up back in the past. I had read Octavia Butler's *Kindred* and had no desire to get into that kind of cycle, assuming it was even something that could happen.

Then I remembered how Martha had called me Jonathan. Maybe that was the name of the guy who looked like me, the guy who apparently was being led to his death by those racists. Martha had loved him. He had loved her.

Martha must've seen Jonathan in me, and that's the reason why she locked onto me like that.

Man, I'm such an ass. I never once considered what she must have been going through seeing someone who looked like the love of her life dating other women. And to add insult to injury, I blocked her from her own room by painting my damn ceiling!

I don't know what I'm going to do, but whatever it is, I'll have to do it soon. Until then, I can't afford to leave this house and risk getting sent back in time.

❦

AFTER STEPHANIE HEARS MY PLAN, she agrees to go to the hardware store to pick me up some white paint. That night I repaint my ceiling. Afterwards, I shower and head to Stephanie's room to sleep. With the window cracked and the fan running, I plan to implement the next part of my plan the following evening.

❦

I AM SITTING on my bed in the dark the following evening when Martha appears.

"You spoke to me once before—on this side," I say.

"Yes," she says. Her voice is almost a whisper inside of my head. I don't know how she is doing this or why she has waited all of this time to talk to me.

"How are you able to do that?"

"You reached out to me and created that bridge, but I didn't want to startle you."

"Well, I feel pretty stupid," I respond.

I can't believe I'm actually having a conversation with Martha, after all of this time. I almost forget I am speaking to a ghost.

"This was your room," I say.

"Yes, it was."

"And I remind you of Jonathan, I assume."

"There's a resemblance," she says, smiling.

"But he's on the other side now. Why are you not with him?"

"I am trapped in this house."

"By what?"

"My anger holds me here—and then I met you."

I sigh. "But I can never be what Jonathan was to you. I am still alive."

"I am not leaving my house!"

Her sharpness scares me for a moment, and I have to settle myself before I continue.

"Are you still able to go to the light?"

"What are you talking about?"

"Can you cross over into heaven or wherever spirits go?"

She smiles. "That's not how it works. My anger has held me here."

"You have to give up that anger. When you showed me your father, I got it. I really did. He was a very bad man, but you have to release that weight."

"No woman will be able to take my place," she says matter-of-factly.

A feeling of hopelessness begins to fill me. "Then I'm leaving. I'm moving out. You can have the house."

"If you leave, I'll take the girl to the other side with me—just like I did you."

"Leave Stephanie out of this. This is between you and me."

"Then you stay!"

My knees become weak, and I sit down on the bed. This wasn't exactly what I had planned. I had just wanted to talk to her, maybe see if she'd lay off. Instead, I'm only angering her further, and from what she's said, that anger is attaching her even further to the house.

But how do you get a ghost to not be angry?

"How did you meet Jonathan?"

This question throws her a little, and she is quiet a moment before she answers. "I met him in town. He was one of the free Negroes who moved here from Baltimore after the war. Very handsome. His father was a Negro doctor."

I nod.

"We noticed each other, and he tipped his hat to me. I smiled and he smiled back." She pauses. "Not everyone was fond of Negroes after the war, but I didn't mind. We fell in love."

"And then your father had him killed?"

She looks at me, and all the pain I had seen in her eyes when she had taken me back in time was there again, fresh on her face.

"And then you got sick," I add.

She looks away. "I was already sick. That's why I didn't care that Daddy knew about my love for Jonathan."

"Did Jonathan know you were sick?"

"Yes. But he didn't care. He was determined to love me."

I lower my head. "I'm very sorry about what happened to you."

Her face softens.

"I have never met anyone like Stephanie before," I say. "This is the first time I have felt I could be happy with someone."

Martha looks at me, as if trying to gage my intentions. "Do you *love* her?"

I take a deep breath. "Nowadays, people take things involving our emotions a little more slowly. But if I were to be completely honest, I can see myself with her many years from now."

"You love her," Martha says.

"I just want the chance to," I respond.

She smiles and her body begins to glow, a sharp yellowish light illuminating her from within. "I love Jonathan."

I nod, finally understanding that we are both allowing ourselves to feel love again.

"Bye, Hawthorne," she says, as her body begins to fade away like fog clearing in late morning.

"Bye, Martha."

And then she's gone. But this time I am no longer frightened at her disappearance.

"You'll have to meet Satchel," I tell Stephanie, as we sit on a bench by one of Port Hilton's many beaches. "We are total opposites, but I think you'd like him."

She smiles, placing her head on my shoulder.

A month has passed since Martha left, and things are back to normal around Wingate House. Mr. Golly and Gunther Pratt are still talking shit. Ms. Grant is still passing gas on her way through the house to her morning meditation in the backyard. Natalie is also preparing to graduate in the spring.

And Stephanie and I? Well, we're exploring the beauty of this new thing that we have found— and if I'm truly honest, it feels a lot like love.

—fin—

ACKNOWLEDGMENTS

I would like to thank the following people for their support throughout this journey:

Mitchell Davis and the Biblioboard family, Sabin Prentis, Jane Friedman, the Black Caucus of the American Library Association, The Virginia Indie Author Project, Dana Evans, Gladys Bell, Nikki Williams, Nia Forrester, Dawayne and Joi Whittington, Richard Wall, Tayari Jones, Victor LaValle, Leslye Penelope, Tananarive Due, Steven Barnes, Erica Buddington, my publishing family at University of Hell Press, my publishing family at Editions Autrement, Kima Jones, Mat Johnson, Jesmyn Ward, Phonte Coleman, Nicolay Rooks, Laurie Carter and the Hampton University department of English and Foreign Languages, Linda Malone-Colon and the office of the School of Liberal Arts and Education (SLAE), Tina Rollins and the staff of the William and Norma Harvey Library, my Blue and White Family of Sigmas and Zetas, and all of the librarians out there making a difference in the world. Also, thanks to Jordan Peele, Donald Glover, and Boots Riley for keeping it strange.

Many thanks to all of my family, wonderfully composed of Walkers, Holbrooks, McGees, Whittleys, Maxies, and Sanderses, with a special thanks to my parents and brother, who have been enthusiastic and vocal supporters of my work for years.

Last, but by no means least, I would like to thank my rock/best friend/love of my life/queen of my small little piece of the universe, Lauren, and my wonderful daughter, Zoë, who continues to amaze and inspire me.

ABOUT THE AUTHOR

Ran Walker is the multi-award-winning author of seventeen books. He teaches creative writing at Hampton University and lives with his wife and daughter in Virginia. He can be reached via his website, www.ranwalker.com.

CPSIA information can be obtained
at www.ICGtesting.com
Printed in the USA
FSHW010000210919
62234FS

9 781020 001000